Acclaim For the Work of
MAX ALLAN COLLINS!

"Max Allan Collins is the closest thing we have to a 21st century Mickey Spillane and…will please any fan of old-school, hardboiled crime fiction."
—*This Week*

"No one can twist you through a maze with as much intensity and suspense as Max Allan Collins."
—*Clive Cussler*

"Collins never misses a beat…All the stand-up pleasures of dime-store pulp with a beguiling level of complexity."
—*Booklist*

"Collins has an outwardly artless style that conceals a great deal of art."
—*New York Times Book Review*

"A suspenseful, wild night's ride [from] one of the finest writers of crime fiction that the U.S. has produced."
—*Book Reporter*

"This book is about as perfect a page turner as you'll find."
—*Library Journal*

"Bristlin̲   book is a welcom̲   library."

She turned around and the nine millimeter was huge in her orange-nailed hand. Her expression was a little crazy.

She said, "You know I could just kill the son of a bitch."

"Not a good idea. Give me that."

"Or maybe you could. Would you kill him for me?" She seemed a little drunk. Maybe that hadn't been her first beer.

"No. That's not a toy."

She handed it to me, with a babyish pout. I took the weapon and held it in both hands; I'd never felt the metal so cold.

She plopped down next to me again. "One of us should kill that miserable prick."

"Yeah, well, not tonight."

Then she got up, suddenly, and ran to the bathroom. When she came back, she positioned herself in front of me.

"How old are you?" she asked.

I told her.

"I was in junior high when you were born," she said.

She took off her sweater, yanked it over her head with magnificent casualness. She stared down at me; so did the bullet bra.

Her hands went behind her to undo the bra. I looked away, the gun still in my hands. This was wrong. I could get in ten kinds of trouble. A hundred. She was a beautiful, sad, troubled woman and she was taking her bra off and I was about to get fucked several ways, not all of them good...

The First
QUARRY

by **Max Allan Collins**

A HARD CASE CRIME NOVEL

A HARD CASE CRIME BOOK
(HCC-048)
October 2008

Published by

Dorchester Publishing Co., Inc.
200 Madison Avenue
New York, NY 10016

in collaboration with Winterfall LLC

*This book is a work of fiction. Names, characters, places, and
incidents either are the products of the author's imagination or
are used fictitiously, and any resemblance to actual events or
persons, living or dead, is entirely coincidental.*

ISBN 0-8439-5965-7
ISBN-13 978-0-8439-5965-9

Cover design by Cooley Design Lab

Typeset by Swordsmith Productions

The name "Hard Case Crime" and the Hard Case Crime logo
are trademarks of Winterfall LLC. Hard Case Crime books are
selected and edited by Charles Ardai.

Printed in the United States of America

Visit us on the web at www.HardCaseCrime.com

To Quarry's old pal,
Gary Meyers

"Fear—jealousy—money—revenge— and protecting someone you love."

**PLAYWRIGHT FREDERICK KNOTT,
LISTING MURDER MOTIVES**
Dial "M" for Murder

DECEMBER 1970

ONE

The night after Christmas and all through the house, it was colder than fuck.

The home was new, brand-new, with the various smells of paint, plastic and disinfectant you might expect. Even the carpet I was sitting on, next to a window onto the quiet street, had a chemical odor. No Christmas decorations lingered here, because the split-level four-bedroom affair was as empty as the boxes littering curbsides across America.

And this was America, all right—Iowa City, Iowa, the heartland, the street out front not really a street at all, but a former county road recently renamed Country Vista, which was ironic because the builders who'd invaded this stretch of farmland-bordered real estate had nothing so much in mind as blotting out a country vista.

Two houses sat on corners on either side of a brand-new lane that made a T with Country Vista, and I sat in one of those houses, the beige split-level on the left as you faced the renamed county road. This new lane had no name yet, just as its dozen split-levels (so far) had no inhabitants; the waiting dwellings squatted on sloping future lawns—snow-pocked dirt right now—with room for an entire development to develop beyond.

This must have pissed off the people across the way no end. The houses opposite had plenty of breathing room, big yards for little cottages, no two alike—from log to stone to brick—with only three visible from my window, even if I craned my neck either direction. Country Vista had once been quiet, even secluded, with trees and bushes and privacy. Right now it still was, though any non-evergreen trees and bushes were skeletal with clumps of white from last week's snowfall.

On the other hand, the people in those varied cottages might not have minded as much as you'd think. I knew the cobblestone cottage almost directly across from my split-level was owned by the university and provided as a perk to a visiting professor, and my best guess was the not-too-nearby neighbors were similarly academics making a temporary home of Iowa City. Or anyway five miles from Iowa City, which is what Country Vista was. So the residents of these cottages were just passing through, and people just passing through can only get so indignant.

The house, my split-level, was indeed cold, but I wasn't, particularly. I'd known that though the electricity was on, the heat wasn't, and that I dared not turn it on or the lights either, nor was hauling in furniture a good idea. In fact, I wasn't even sleeping here—I was making use of a Holiday Inn just four miles away. But I had brought in a space heater and that was keeping things nice and toasty. I had thermal underwear from JC Penney and a thermos of hot chocolate filled at a 7-Eleven (coffee is for grown-ups) where I'd also purchased some plastic-wrapped sandwiches, turkey and cheese, ham and cheese.

Not a bad set-up.

I wondered what cops did, when they had to do surveillance this time of year. Maybe in a big city it wouldn't be a big deal, sitting in a car with the engine going; but in a college town like Iowa City, and particularly on a quiet country lane like Country Vista, you would stick out like some asshole sitting in his car doing surveillance.

As far as Iowa City itself went, I didn't stick out at all. I certainly didn't look like a guy who'd come to town to take out a college professor. And by "take out," I don't mean invite to dinner—I was here to put a bullet in the brain (or heart, my option) of a supposedly fairly well-known writer called K.J. Byron. This was a contract kill, and I was the contract killer, even if I looked like just another college kid.

My hair wasn't as long as most of the guys in this town, but it was longer than it had been, not so long ago. You see while the kids in Iowa City were going to college, I had gone to Vietnam, where I had unwittingly learned a trade. I'd been a sniper, but this job would require close-up work, which was fine. Dead is dead.

Funny thing, the only kids wearing Army khaki or camouflage were hippies, sometimes painting peace symbols on their back or whatever. Any returning vets going to school on Uncle Sugar wouldn't be caught dead in military gear, although plenty had been caught wounded in it. Certainly my hair wasn't long enough to pass as one of the Make Love Not War crowd, so I probably looked more preppie or frat boy in my sweaters and blue jeans and corduroy jacket. Only the heavy boots might have given me away, but in Iowa this time of year, not really.

No one, including you, would have made me for any kind of killer, not even one recently back from Nam. The brown hair, long enough to touch my ears, the baby face, the one-hundred-fifty-five pounds on a five ten frame, were nothing threatening, and mine was a face in the crowd.

Of course there wasn't much of a crowd in a college town during Christmas break. Only local kids right now, and foreign students, and the handful who for whatever reason hadn't gone home for mistletoe and holly, by gosh by golly. Older students with apartments might spend a handful of holiday days with Mom and Dad, and would be home soon. But a downtown hopping with bars and boutiques and record stores and head shops that was usually crawling with college kids wasn't.

I'm not what you'd call a people person, so that didn't bother me, other than wishing I had additional nonentities around to blend in with. I could have used more hair on my face—these hirsute hippies at least had an excuse in this cold—but if I stopped in for a beer and a burger somewhere, I fit in fine. A university is big enough that nobody, not even a bartender, wonders why they haven't seen you before.

I had arrived this morning, having flown into Cedar

Rapids where I rented a car, a little dark blue Ford Maverick. Iowa City was a half hour drive. I'd checked into the Holiday Inn and had purchased a few things, including the space heater, at a nearby Kmart. I already knew I'd be squatting in that split-level; I even had a key to the place.

Parking in the driveway or pulling into the garage might have aroused suspicion, right across from the target's residence. The Broker—more about him later —had provided me with a second set of keys that had allowed me to park in the garage of the empty finished home behind mine. I'd been told I could risk camping out in either house, if I didn't mind the cold. Well, I minded the cold; even a Holiday Inn is preferable to cold.

But I did find it interesting that the Broker had all these keys. He knew things, all sorts of things, and my surveillance was only designed for the most basic fact-finding—specifically, what pattern did Professor Byron maintain over the Christmas break.

Establishing the pattern of a target is key, particularly if collateral damage is undesirable, and let me be frank: collateral damage is where I draw the line. I was willing to protect myself with the death of an innocent bystander, if my survival was at stake; but going around killing people willy-nilly was for psychopaths, not professionals.

Collateral Damage, oddly enough, was the name of a book Professor Byron had written, a so-called non-fiction novel about death by friendly fire in Vietnam. I hadn't read the book or heard of it, either, but the Broker said it was a bestseller and a pretty big deal. Supposedly the professor had written several critically acclaimed novels that had stiffed but was now making a new name for himself with this non-fiction novel dodge, and I say dodge because I never went to college but I know novels aren't non-fiction.

Before I had taken this job—not the job of taking out the prof, but the job itself, of killing people for money —I had done a certain amount of soul searching. I had learned to kill in the jungle of Vietnam and figured I could kill in the zoo of America just as easily. When you take somebody out with a sniper scope, though, or you return fire in a rice paddy fire fight, that's self-defense, even if a sniper represents a preemptive kind of self-defense.

A professional killer taking out a target isn't self-defense, obviously; but I didn't figure killing somebody who was already dead was anything I couldn't live with. Because anybody that somebody else had decided needed to be killed was already dead, at least when that somebody else was powerful enough and determined enough to go the extra yard and hire a killer.

And yet I wouldn't be the killer, not really. I'd just be the mechanism. The killer had hired the job. And if it wasn't me, it would be somebody else getting paid. And fuck somebody else, anyway.

Now the Broker had provided the target's pattern. Somebody had been in before me to do surveillance, and had taken it all down, and I'd been provided with the data. But it was pretty worthless—the Broker knew that—and I'd been told I'd have to basically start from scratch. The hope was that the prof's life during the uncharted territory of his Christmas break would be leisurely. Maybe he'd burrow in and write a book or something.

No such luck.

I had taken a chance and got started at dusk, parking the Maverick in the garage of the split-level behind my surveillance post (as per instruction), and I had barely settled in at the window, my thermos nearby, a little portable radio quietly playing an FM station that mixed hits with album cuts, when the first female showed up at the cobblestone cottage.

She was driving a little red Fiat and was small and fair and pretty in a Breck Girl kind of way. I took her for a blonde but truth be told she had on a rabbit-fur hat that looked like a beehive hairdo gone wacky (wackier) and I couldn't see any hair except for dark eyebrows. Her coat was light green corduroy with a rabbit collar like the hat and she had similarly fur-trimmed tan suede boots with heels. Her legs were black, or that is, her leggings were.

I shut off the radio and cranked the window open enough to let in the cold and some outside sound.

The way she slammed the car door, you just knew she was pissed off. Then she tromped up the graduated cement sidewalk with similar irritated determination; up on the little stoop, she opened the storm door and then her tan-gloved right fist hammered the dark wood of the front door like she was driving a nail. There was a brass knocker, but she apparently preferred hammering.

She paused, waited for ten seconds, then hammered some more.

Nothing.

I knew the prof was in there—I'd seen him moving around through the front room windows, whose curtains were open.

Then the girl—and she *was* a girl, maybe nineteen—noticed those windows herself and came down off the stoop to tippy-toe at the evergreen bushes to peek in. She seemed to see nothing. Then she strode across the front yard, arms pistoning, pretty little jaw firm, stopped to look in a window of the little free-standing cobblestone garage where the prof kept his Volvo, then disappeared around the house.

I heard some more hammering. I took a bite of turkey and Swiss—pretty bad. Thin slices of would-be meat and processed cheese that took more chewing than cheese really should. I swigged at a Coke—I'd brought a few cans along, for the caffeine, and they stayed cold outside of space heater range—and let its sweetness wash away the bad sandwich. Some more hammering.

Then she came marching around the house on the other side, looking like a soldier in a high school operetta with that high furry hat—you could thank *Doctor Zhivago* for this shit, I supposed—and she made her way up onto the porch.

She did not hammer.

She screamed: *"I know you're in there, you prick!"*

I smiled to myself. Nibbled some more sandwich. With a show to watch, it went down better.

"You fucking, *cock*-sucking *prick!"*

I laughed a little. I liked her. But I had a feeling she wasn't a major player in the melodrama I'd just been inserted into. This was the tail end of her performance, I figured, based upon the surveillance info the Broker gave me.

I was right.

"You mother-*fucking*, dick-*licking* son of a fucking *bitch!"*

I recalled how much trouble a girl I'd known in junior high had got into when she told a friend of hers, who'd moved in on her guy, to go to hell between classes. A week of detention, and lucky not to be expelled. Things had changed in a very few years in this country.

The door opened, not at all tentatively, in fact with a suddenness that showed the novelist had a non-fictional way of making a point. He was tall and he was skinny, a handsome Ichabod Crane, his face narrow and well-carved with a hawkish nose the dominant feature, his hair dark blonde and shaggy but not hippie-length, his eyebrows unruly. He was wearing a maroon terry-cloth bathrobe, belt knotted at the waist, with a white t-shirt peeking out, and his legs were bare, his feet in slippers.

He looked side to side, perhaps to see if any neighbors were observing this little scene, but his neighbors were well away from him and of course he had no idea I was spying.

He said, "Is this really *necessary*, Alice? Haven't we *said* our goodbyes?"

I think that was what he said. He was speaking at a normal level, and I was across the street, but the clear cold air carried well, and he had a lecture-room baritone.

"You *bastard!*" she said, and she started pounding on his chest with both gloved fists, at least as hard as she'd hammered the door.

He took her by the shoulders and held her out away from him like an archeologist appraising a find. His arms were long and she was petite. She was screaming at him, no words, not even obscenities, and he shook her, hard, the way you might a child, if you were a sucky parent, anyway.

Turned out I was right, she was a blonde: he shook that rabbit-fur hat right off her head. She had lots of blonde hair, long and flowing, and from my perch she seemed a real doll. But from my perch I knew the prof had already moved on: advance surveillance info indicated Byron's latest conquest as being a brunette on the tall side, specifically a grad student in his creative writing class name of Annette Girard.

"What we did I'll never forget," he told her, clasping her by the arms, working in compassion and regret the way a cook might sprinkle paprika. "But I'm a married man and twice your age. Let's cherish what we have, and go back to our lives."

She said something that I couldn't quite make out; more a whimper than speech, really, but I got the feeling she said she wanted to come in.

That was her best card—she had to play it. If she could get the prof inside that house, then inside her, she was back in the game. I wondered if she knew about the brunette.

"What do you *see* in that cunt, anyway? She's a *stick!* She's a *skinny* fucking *stick!*"

Apparently she knew about the brunette.

"I'm Annette's faculty advisor," he said, "and her teacher. She is also my teaching assistant. What we had, you and I, Alice...was special. Unique. My relationship with Annette is strictly...teacher-pupil."

"Right! *Cocksucking* 101!"

"That's enough." He took her by the arm and he marched her down the stoop's stairs and the sidewalk, practically dragging her, his bathrobe flapping, belt coming undone, skinny bare legs showing. Her eyes were like a raccoon's, black-ringed hysteria, the mascara wet and running. Her lips were trembling.

Now she was saying, "I love you, I love you, I love you, I love you," how many times I lost count.

At her car, he looked to his left but not to his right —this I took not to be checking on the neighbors but seeing if anybody was coming from the main drag half a mile or so down. I got the impression this scene with Alice was not one he would like Annette to come in on.

Then it occurred to me that Alice and Annette were both A's, and were in alphabetical order, at that. Maybe

Professor Hefner was working his way through his female students. If so, he was using the second semester list, and starting over. This stud would have covered more ground in the first semester than just a couple of damn A's.

He deposited her in the car, though the driver's side door remained open. "Can you drive?"

She responded, behind the wheel, but I couldn't hear it.

"I tell you what. At the end of the school year, when you've graduated, when seeing each other would be more appropriate…we'll talk again."

Her body straightened as hope sprung. This I could hear: "Really? *Really*, my darling?"

My darling motherfucking, dick-licking son of a fucking bitch?

"Yes. It will be hard for us…"

Right. This prick was always hard.

"…but we'll wait, until you're twenty-one, and a college graduate. And if you go on for your MFA? Perhaps I'll need a *new* teaching assistant.…"

This seemed to please her, and he leaned in and gave her a kiss. At least I think that's what he did—couldn't quite make it out, though it lasted a while and was not just a peck. I could only wonder why Alice hadn't realized he was tacitly admitting that he boinked his teaching assistants, but logic was never that big in Wonderland.

He shut her in the little red car and she drove off, and he watched, and waved, and smiled, and then the smile drooped and he shivered, not with the cold I didn't think, and he stooped his shoulders and trod back up and inside his cobblestone cottage.

Killing this fucker wouldn't lose me any sleep. I finished my Coke and leaned back against the rolled-up sleeping bag I'd brought with me. Like I said, I didn't figure to spend any of the nights here, but that option was good to have and, anyway, the sleeping bag rolled up made a nice soft object to rest against.

Twilight turned to honest-to-shit night and a couple of street lamps—well-spaced—came on. Though I sat in a split-level, the world across the way was woodsy and rustic with those quaint-looking cottages like something out of another era.

Around seven, "American Woman" was on the radio, throbbing despite the low volume, when the white Corvette pulled up. I turned the sound down to zero and watched, impressed, as the tall brunette unfolded from a vehicle that should have been splashed with winter grue but was showroom shiny. She'd taken time to run it through a car wash, I'd bet, as careful with her wheels as with her own appearance.

And she was careful with her appearance, all right. Her coat was white leather with a white fur collar, her long legs in black-and-white geometrically patterned bell bottoms, her boots white leather with heels. Her long dark hair went halfway down her back, straight as a waterfall, the mane of a lanky lioness. Her complexion was olive, almost tan, whether from some vacation she'd grabbed or just her natural state, I couldn't say.

Alice had been cute, perky, if psychotic. Annette was a different animal, and not the short, plump

Italian Mouseketeer Frankie Avalon had tried to beach ball. This was a fashion-model type, her oval face, her full dark-lipsticked mouth, her big brown eyes, her well-shaped dark eyebrows, a study in symmetry.

Teaching assistant my ass.

He came down out of the cottage to meet her, and the bathrobe had been replaced by a tan leisure suit with a brown shirt with one of those collars that could put an eye out. Both eyes.

He came down, his breath pluming in the cold— the temperature had dropped some—and slipped an arm around her shoulders and led her up and inside. She had a little brown briefcase with her, so perhaps they were just going to work.

Three hours later they were still in there.

I probably shouldn't have done it, but I was getting bored. Surveillance was not what I'd bargained for, though the Broker had made it clear sitting watch would come into play from time to time in this line of work. Anyway, I was getting bored and itchy and frankly curious.

So I stuffed the nine millimeter in my waistband, zipped the cord jacket over it, and went out the back way and cut through some undeveloped wooded property until I could cross the street a quarter of a mile away, and come up behind the cobblestone house and peek in a window or two.

Which is exactly what I did.

They were in a small room that I would best describe as a study—lots of books on shelves, and a big rolltop desk littered with more books and manuscript pages and a typewriter with a ream of white typing paper next to it. That's where he was sitting.

So maybe they *were* working, right?

Well, she was anyway. She was in pink panties on her knees, blowing the guy, his leisure suit pants around his ankles.

Fuck, I would have killed this lucky prick for free.

TWO

I have a pretty good memory. I can recall conversations well, at least well enough to write them down for your benefit and have them pass muster. Same is true of people, their physical descriptions and the sounds of their voices and even what they were wearing—it all seems to stick.

But I don't remember the exact words when the Broker came around to that little two-room apartment and recruited me for his team, even though it was one of the more important conversations of my life.

That was a bad period for me. For the month or so I'd been living in a rough patch of L.A., alternating between staying in bed feeling sorry for myself, watching daytime TV (game shows, not soaps), eating TV dinners, and venturing forth looking for women who were willing to fuck me for free, even if a certain venereal after-fee might get tacked on.

I was also drinking heavily, which is something I don't normally do. In fact, I am more a soft drink kind of guy, though I do like wine, on special occasions, like New Year's Eve or getting back from Vietnam.

And getting back from Vietnam is where I should start, really, to fill you in a little on how I became somebody who killed people for money. Or I should say somebody who killed people for good money, be-

cause in Nam I killed people for shit change, didn't I?
And the only person I ever killed for free was probably
the only one that really counted, the only one that really
mattered, and that I truly enjoyed doing.

Before I went over, I'd been stationed on the West
Coast, and that's where I met the California girl who
became my bride. It was one of those whirlwind ro-
mances that are passionate and romantic and run to
montages in the movies where the couples are hand in
hand on the beach and in the park and share one ice
cream cone with pop songs playing in the background.
In our case it would have been something by the Asso-
ciation, "Cherish" maybe, though "No Fair At All"
would have been more like it.

Because when I got home to our little bungalow in
La Mirada, a day early, meaning to surprise my darling
girl, I got surprised myself because she was in bed
with a guy named Williams. I didn't know his name
was Williams at the time, but when I asked around the
neighborhood later that day, I got filled in fast. He
lived in La Mirada, too, just a couple blocks away,
which is one reason why his car wasn't in my sweetie's
driveway.

Another reason was that, at the moment, his car
wasn't running right. The next morning he and it were
in his own driveway, Williams under the spiffy little
sportscar, on his back working on its rear end—a coincidence, because the day before he'd been working on
my wife's rear end—and he looked up at me from
under there, the buggy jacked up with the back wheels
off, and gave me this look, which I read as contemp-

tuous, and commented, "I got nothing to say to you, bunghole," which didn't take much reading at all, and I said, "Fine," and kicked out the fucking jack.

That almost caused me some trouble. Had I killed the prick still in the sack with my wife, I'd have been in a better position to claim temporary insanity and irresistible impulse and suchlike. Instead, after I'd found them together in what I'd presumed was my bed, I'd walked off and settled down and thought about it overnight and gone around to his house the next day and crushed the fucker under his car.

That got me arrested, though I explained that if I'd gone over there to do anything but talk, I would have taken a gun. I'd killed his ass, all right, but it wasn't premeditated. He'd just gotten on my wrong side, calling me a bunghole and being generally disrespectful, and the thing hadn't been planned. Not calculated at all. It was just he said "Fuck you" in his way and I said "Fuck you" in mine—only mine took on a more physical form.

The media had a whale of a time with it, and the public was on my side, so there was no trial. The war wasn't popular, sure, but Johnny couldn't be expected to come marching home and not get pissed off catching some son of a bitch fucking his wife. So the D.A. dropped it, saying it would be a waste of the taxpayers' money, and then some fuss followed, since a public servant can't really win in a situation like that. Damned if you do....

Only there was a backlash against me. I couldn't find work, not that I was qualified for anything except shooting yellow people from atop brown trees between green fronds. Sure, I'd worked in garages as a high school kid and was a pretty good pick-up mechanic, certainly qualified to pump gas and learn on the job. But nobody was interested, not even where Williams used to work as a mechanic, and it wasn't like they didn't have an opening.

By the way, I had nothing to do with my wife after that. At this point I didn't want to kill her any more than I wanted to fuck her (though fuck her and kill her had flashed through my mind as an option, on reflection not a terribly good one) and she divorced me. Hey, she had grounds.

The first week I was in that little two-room shithole, my old man came out from Ohio and looked me up. We'd had a pretty good relationship over the years; I'd lettered in swimming in high school and that had pleased him (he'd been an athlete in college). I maintained a B average and I didn't get any girls pregnant, which was the very definition of a good kid. He was out of town on business a lot, so we weren't maybe as close as some fathers and sons. But we didn't hate each other, like a lot of my friends and their dads.

He'd hit a bad slump around 1967 in his business—he had a little real estate agency—and that had made putting me through college a non-starter. He advised me to enlist and then I'd have Uncle Sam's help with college, and that seemed like a good idea at the time.

Anyway, he knew about the trouble I'd been in, even though it didn't hit the national press, and came to see me with a very special message: "Don't come home." He would have been cool with it, but my step-mother (a wealthy widow he'd snagged who'd made his business worries go away) had found me off-putting even before I started kicking jacks out.

"You're a man," he'd said. "You understand about women."

I almost said, *Why don't you reflect on my current situation, Dad, and see if you still think I understand about women.* But I didn't.

"I just want you to know," he said right before he departed my fleabag Shangri-la, "I'm proud of what you did in the service of your country."

So killing a bunch of Cong who were strangers to me, squeezing off rounds and shattering and splattering their noggins like melons at target practice back home, that was fine, that made sense. Killing that prick Williams, who had needed killing, who I had a reason for killing, that was wrong.

That may have been when the gears shifted in my skull and made me view things from my own admittedly off-kilter perspective. Society sanctioned killing strangers in war, but didn't like it when you took out some bastard you knew who richly deserved it. To me that's hypocritical, but what the hell, that's just my take on it.

So the Broker.

He knocked on my door. At that stage in my existence, I didn't even bother to take a gun with me. This joint couldn't afford peepholes, either, so I just opened the door and there he stood, an apparition of success: six two and broad-shouldered, with stark-white hair made starker by a tropical tan and a gray double-knit suit and a darker stripes of gray tie, as distinguished as a guy in a bourbon ad in *Playboy*.

He called me "Mister," and used my real name, which is none of your fucking business. He had the damnedest face, too young for the white hair, long and fleshy but largely unlined, and his eyes were light blue, like arctic waters, or anyway like I figured arctic waters would look.

I do remember he said, "I have an unusual opportunity for you, Mr. _____. A money-making opportunity."

And I remember my answer: "Amway's not my thing, Mac. Try next door. There's a hooker with some real sales experience."

But he talked his way in, and we sat at the little scarred-up table where I had my TV dinners and the rum I was mixing with Coca-Cola, a twelve-ounce can of Coke lasting longer than a bottle of Bacardi.

I took him for forty, despite the white hair, but came to find out fifty was more like it. He had the manner of a well-heeled lawyer or maybe a politician, and I do recall he began with a fairly lengthy diatribe on how poorly I'd been treated by, well, just about everybody—my wife, the press, the legal system, even my family, and how the hell did he know that?

Another thing I remember is the chill I felt, when I realized this guy had researched me. Who was I, for anybody to look into me? But the Broker had it all down, chapter and verse, and now it gets vague in my memory. He didn't come straight out and ask me if I was interested in killing people for hire, of course not;

it was more like, *How would you like to make real money at home doing what you did for almost no money overseas?*

Looking back, I was ripe for the Broker. I might have gone in any direction about then. Maybe if that *had* been Amway at the door, or the Jehovah's Witnesses, I'd have gone off into some other form of lunacy. But it was the Broker who caught me at just the right time, thank God.

And, anyway, Amway or the Witnesses wouldn't have offered me an advance of fifty thousand dollars. That was attractive to a guy living in two dingy rooms. So was the notion that half a dozen jobs a year would bring in another fifteen thousand or so; and when the fifty K had earned out (I'd be getting only half of each fee till it was), I'd be at thirty a year, minimum. The average yearly income for an honest man was under ten grand.

I would have a bogus job to pay taxes for, though I wouldn't have to record my real income, the bulk of which would be in cash. I would be a salesman with a sample case and could even call on clients if need be, to establish a cover. My wares? Lingerie. That made the Broker smile, and I smiled, too, but just to be nice.

The Broker, you see, was "a sort of an agent," a middleman in the murder business, insulation between client and killer. I would not know the client's name, and the client would not know mine.

That had been two months ago. In the meantime I had bought a house, a little pre-fab A-frame cottage on a small lake in Wisconsin. When summer rolled around, that lake would be nice to swim in, but in the meantime I joined the YMCA at nearby Lake Geneva, and swam every day. It was my only exercise and perhaps my only passion. It relaxed me, and helped me think, when I was so inclined, but didn't demand it of me, if I wasn't.

The A-frame was perfect for my needs. This particular lake was underdeveloped and I had a lot of privacy, though I anticipated the warm months would be anything but private. On the other hand, that Lake Geneva was a vacation area suited me. I liked the idea of having access to good-looking college girls who could come and go. I got a kick out of the Playboy Club, and would dress up a little and get that James Bond vibe on, Bunnies dipping to serve up a drink and a view of the hills of heaven, name entertainers taking the stage, and the food a big step up from what I could rustle up for myself.

Life at the A-frame was dull and that suited me fine. I had television, although the reception was poor and I would eventually have to put in an antenna half the size of the place, and I liked to read, Harold Robbins and paperback westerns and science fiction, mostly, nothing heavy. I was living a life of leisure and started thinking the Broker was just this crazy asshole who went around spreading demented stories and piles of cash. Like that guy on TV when I was a kid—the Millionaire. Writes you a check and then disappears. Cool.

But the Broker didn't disappear. He called and summoned me; I felt like I'd been tapped for jury duty.

I had a little green Opel GT that had cost me about four grand of that fifty Broker had given me, and I drove it to the Iowa/Illinois Quad Cities, specifically Davenport, where as per instructions I checked into a ten-story hotel called the Concort Inn near the government bridge. The Broker either owned the place or had a piece of the action—at least that was my theory. Because he seemed to feel perfectly comfortable meeting with me openly at the hotel, even housing me there.

I liked the hotel. The room I'd been provided was spacious, nicely furnished in an anonymous modern way, with a view of the Mississippi River where you could see the other cities across the way. The television reception was outstanding, and the room service wasn't bad, either. The swimming pool was medium-size and the water was too warm, but nice to have, anyway.

You might think the Broker would come to my room to confab, but on this occasion, at least, he had me meet him in the lounge downstairs, a Gay '90s-theme bar with a modest nightclub-style dance floor and stage. At 3:30 p.m., the place was closed and we had the whole room to ourselves, just us and the gaudy San Francisco whorehouse decor. Broker was already ensconced in a red faux-leather button-tufted booth, his double-knit suit tan, his wide silk tie shades of tan and brown.

He was organized, the Broker. A pot of coffee for him and a glass of ice with two bottles of Coke waiting at my seat. The bottles were unopened, but of course

an opener on a napkin was nearby. On Broker's side of
the table, a pack of Viceroys and a gold Zippo and an
ashtray were poised for his use.

The baritone was warm and mellow: "Accommo-
dations suit you, Quarry?"

That was the name Broker had started calling me.
Whether it was a first name or last never came up—
but the Broker was usually polite, so the absence of a
"mister" in front of it may have indicated first. I had a
feeling it was a sort of code name for the Broker, who
did have a cute streak—a single-o, like Liberace or
Tarzan or Cher.

Or Broker.

"Swell," I said. "Pretty nice hotel, considering the
neighborhood."

A seedy warehouse district was nearby.

The Broker shrugged. "The traffic flow is ideal, and
with the bridge right here? People who come to the
Cities with business to do at the Arsenal find it most
convenient."

The Rock Island Arsenal was a major employer in
the Quad Cities. I figured I was right—the Broker had
a piece of this place, otherwise why the knee-jerk
puff job?

I glanced around at the red brocade wallpaper; you
could see people moving out in the kitchen through
windows in steel doors. "This is a little public, isn't it?
Not exactly where I expected us to meet."

He waved a hand heavy with gold and diamonds in
Pope-like benediction. "There'll be no dark alleys,
Quarry. We're business associates. No need for para-

noia, discretion suffices. I have enough clout around here that we can meet in comfort and relative seclusion without having to resort to ridiculously surreptitious measures."

"Yeah, that would suck."

He was studying me. His smile went up and his white mustache drooped down. A hundred years ago, this was a man who'd have bought and sold slaves. But I wasn't perfect, either.

He said, "Judging by your confident demeanor, I would say you've had no second thoughts about the direction of our business relationship."

"I spent a bunch of the money," I said. I worked the opener on one of the Cokes and it made a *pop*. I could say it sounded like a gunshot, for dramatic effect, but it didn't, really. "So I'm in. There's a job?"

"A *first* job," he said, and he chuckled, as if he were about to tell his twelve-year-old son about the birds and the bees. "And the first job is of course the most important."

"Really? I'd think the final job."

His brow furrowed. "And I do wish, right out of the gate like this, that I had something…*simple* for you. Something straightforward and not at all complex. Although I admit seeing how you handle a challenge will be instructive all around."

I frowned. "My understanding was that my role would always be pretty straightforward. And never complex."

The Broker reached for the pack of cigarettes and selected one and lighted it up with the golden Zippo.

"Life is inherently complex. The human organism itself is complex, with enough moving parts to make the inner workings of a Swiss watch seem about as complicated as a slingshot. And human relationships…my God, they are even more complex than that!"

"Death isn't." I sipped Coke. "It's just a switch that gets turned off."

A white eyebrow lifted in the tan face. "You are correct, Quarry. Unarguably correct. Each death, each killing, is inherently simple, a mere stoppage…but *you* will not be not dead, Quarry, after you've done your fatal work: you must live to kill another day, even though you are caught up in the complexities of the life that you've just taken, complexities that continue on after death—and I speak not of the decay of the flesh, rather the remnants of human relationships."

Did I mention he was a pompous motherfucker?

He was saying, "A switch you turn off, you say, that's what death is. Fine. Let's accept that premise. So you turn off a switch on the second floor of a house with which you're unfamiliar—what do you do? You stumble in the dark. Perhaps you fall down a flight of stairs to your own death."

"You're saying this is not about blundering in, pulling a trigger, and blundering out."

"Correct."

"Well, I know that." I shrugged and poured some more Coke. "I learned this particular skill taking part in missions that were well-thought-out."

"Really? How *is* that war going?"

Well, he had a point.

He exhaled smoke. Then he sipped coffee. And smiled. How could that fucking smile be so white with all the cigarettes and coffee he sucked down? Too complex for me.

"Quarry," he said, damn near purring, "the act itself may indeed be simple—a trigger is pulled, a heart is ripped apart, a skull is shattered and the brain within turned to useless sludge. But what leads up to the act does indeed take care and precision and information. Not unlike a military operation, as you indicated."

"Okay," I said.

The blue eyes gave me a laser look. "In the future, you will be paired with another member of my little army."

I shook my head. "Not what we talked about. I work alone."

He turned a hand over. "Actually, this time you *will* work alone. You may do several jobs alone before I team you with another. That is, in part, a precaution on my part."

"I don't need protecting."

"Perhaps not, but *I* do." He sipped coffee, then gazed at me coldly. "I am not risking an employee into whom I've invested time and money and effort and energy on a…new recruit, shall we say. You will have to prove yourself in the field before I pair you up with a partner, a partner of *my* choice."

I was frowning. None of this had come up in his sales pitch. "Why the hell would I need a partner?"

His eyebrows lifted in a facial shrug; we might have been discussing a sales campaign for this year's model whatever-the-fuck. "The way our contracts are carried out is a time-proven technique and a painstaking approach that I am pleased to say has never yet resulted in either an arrest or death for any of my associates."

Later I would come to question this assertion, but at that moment, I felt reassured by it, and I stopped fighting the notion of working with somebody else, at least long enough to let him explain himself.

Which he did: "Each contract initiates a two-pronged effort. First, a man goes in and quietly gathers information, primarily through established surveillance techniques. We will spend as much as a month getting down the pattern of a target, and never less than a week. We are preparing for a surgical strike, and we need to know when the time is right for getting in and getting out without any collateral damage."

"That I like," I admitted. "I don't want to go around killing innocent people. I'm not some sick fuck."

A smile twitched under the mustache, which itself stayed steady. "Good. You seem already to understand the basic tenet of this business, and of your craft—these individuals we target are…well, let me back up: *we* do not target them. Others target them, and once these individuals have been targeted, they are already dead. They are obituaries waiting to be written. We have nothing to do with their deaths, other than the trivial detail of how those deaths are carried out."

"Because these are inevitable deaths," I said.

A crisp nod. "Correct. These are terminal cases before we ever get on the scene. You're a surgeon removing a tumor."

"I just won't have much of a recovery rate."

That made him smile a little. "Not true—those whose lives our targets afflicted will be free from their misery. Our *clients* are the patients in this medical metaphor, not the targets, who would in this case be the tumors."

"I get it," I said. "I did okay in English."

Did I mention he was a pretentious windbag?

"Normally, you would go in for the last few days of surveillance, and be briefed in person and in detail by your partner, who would remain to provide back-up in the event something might go less than smoothly."

"By goes less than smoothly, you mean, gets fucked up."

"Yes. But as I say, we have a flawless record."

I sipped Coke. Studied him. "Only on this job, this first job, I go in alone?"

He nodded. "We've had a man on the scene for over a month—he'll have left by the time you get there. You don't have any plans for Christmas, do you?"

"Just singing carols at orphanages and old folks homes, why?"

As if I hadn't been kidding, he said, "But you'll be free on the day after?"

"Yeah. I should have all my good works polished off by then."

His eyes seemed sleepy suddenly, half-lidded, though his tone was crisp, the mellow baritone taking on an edge: "You'll go in on the twenty-sixth. Don't drive your own vehicle. Never drive your own vehicle, always rent. You'll fly out of Chicago."

I was pouring myself more Coca-Cola. "You said this was complex. What's complex about it?"

A jaw muscle twitched. "You have to do more than just eliminate the target."

"Isn't that enough?"

"Normally. But in this instance, the target has made a real nuisance of himself. You'll need to find some documents."

"And deliver them to you?"

"No, destroy them. You can burn them in the fireplace of the cottage where your target lives."

"Good thing it's the day *after* Christmas, then."

"Oh?"

I grinned at him. "Would hate to singe Santa."

He just looked at me. Then he smiled, big, taking the mustache along for the ride this time. "Very droll, Quarry," he said. "Very droll."

"That's what it said in my high school yearbook, Broker—Most Likely to Be Droll. Now, who do I have to kill?"

THREE

That first night camped out in the split-level turned into morning—three in the morning, actually—before I decided that my non-Mouseketeer Annette would be spending the night in the cobblestone cottage with her favorite professor, tuckered out after her oral exams.

I admit that I had considered several scenarios designed to bring this assignment to its desired conclusion and right away. None of these, however, suited the Broker's mandate of care and caution, and mostly included me going over there and somehow dealing non-violently (or anyway non-fatally) with the brunette, and then snuffing the prof, finding the manuscript pages Broker wanted destroyed, destroying them, and heading back to the lake and my A-frame to wait for money and praise to arrive from the Broker.

Some of these scenarios were pretty fanciful, involving chloroforming the girl (where would I get that stuff, exactly—a heist at the University hospital?) or knocking her out gently, like they do on TV, only in real-life that kind of blow kills you half the time. Pretty much all of these idiot plans had me shooting the prof multiple times, watching him shake, rattle and roll in *Wild Bunch* slow motion while I grinned maniacally. Somehow this didn't seem in line with the Broker's low-key wishes.

What was my problem, anyway?

What was the philandering Byron to me? Why did I care how many coeds blew and/or boffed him? I was generally in favor of girls blowing and boffing guys, although old farts like the prof (fucker was pushing forty) getting blown and boffed by young girls made me a little queasy, admittedly. I mean, there are limits.

So part of why I threw in the towel at three a.m. on my first stakeout was a sense that I needed rest and refreshment of my faculties, and anyway I did not want to fall asleep in this cold house where my pants could catch fire being too close to the space heater while the rest of me froze its nuts off.

By three-thirty I was in my Holiday Inn Room all snuggled up in my wee little bed. I didn't need a lot of sleep and woke up around eight-thirty a.m. The window view told me that snow had fallen during my slumber and the world was a winter wonderland out there, thick fluffy stuff and evergreen trees plump with white, but the plows had been out, so you could go and enjoy Jack Frost's handiwork without winding up dead in a ditch.

I showered, threw on a sweater and jeans and went down for breakfast. The motel was pretty dead—this was the Sunday after Christmas and the usual businessman clientele were not on the road and the other guests seemed to be made up of family members who were overflow from the homes of relatives who'd run out of spare rooms.

That meant that later, around ten, when I went down for a swim, I had to share the chlorine-scented echo chamber with squealing, splashing kids, whose shrill glee would have sent a guy with a hangover looking for a drill press to squash his head in. But I didn't have a hangover, or a drill press for that matter, and anyway didn't hate children any more than the next guy, so I settled into the whirlpool bath and let the hot, churning water soothe me.

A woman who presumably was the mother of at least one or two of the eight or nine turning the swimming pool room into a combination day care center and horror show padded over in a bright orange one-piece swimsuit. She'd put on a little weight having kiddies, but there was no doubt why somebody had wanted to have kiddies with her in the first place—she was a redhead with an Afro-ish tower of permed but tousled hair and a roundish pleasant face and displayed the kind of curvy frame that makes you really lenient about cellulite.

She settled in across from me. In ten years, she wouldn't rate a second look. But right now the way her full breasts hit the top of the water and the crinkles around her dark blue eyes as she smiled at the pleasure the water jet at her back was giving her was giving me a hard on. The hard on was safely beneath the water, not causing anybody any trouble, not even me, but I wondered what the hell was wrong with my ass. A woman almost ten years older than me, tending her kiddies at a pool, had my dick throbbing.

I was supposed to be in control. Last night, or early this morning I guess would be more accurate, I had considered wild scenarios that had me behaving like a lunatic in carrying out a job that required cautious planning and detached professionalism. What the fuck was wrong with me?

The bubbling water and the kiddie shrieks played like dissonant modern music as I sat there with my arms winged on the concrete lip of the whirlpool, smiling at the redheaded mom, whose posture mirrored mine.

"Have a nice Christmas?" she asked.

"You bet."

"Get everything you wanted?"

She couldn't see my erection, could she? I had boxer-type trunks on that billowed with the water, so I should be safe, though when the bubbles turned off, I could be sitting here with a tent in my lap.

I said, "I guess no kid gets everything he wants."

"Oh, so you're a kid, huh?"

"Overgrown."

"Like all men," she said, and she grinned, nice white teeth, kind of big, a very real smile that wasn't at all practiced.

"Which of these kids are yours?"

"What? None of them."

"Oh." Actually, more like: "Oh!" Not out of surprise (though everything I'd assumed about her had just gone poof), but the need to talk above the frothing hot tub and the screaming brats. Pretty much everything we were saying rated an exclamation point, only you'll have to fill that in yourself.

She said, "So aren't you going to ask me what a nice girl like me is doing in a place like this?"

"I didn't want to pry."

She slid around and sat next to me. Not right next to me, but a more intimate arrangement for sure, though still requiring shouted conversation.

"My name's Dorrie," she said, and she offered a hand with red-painted nails.

I froze for a second, wondering if I was supposed to kiss it; not being a fucking Frenchman, I just shook it. I was really nervous, because my erection had grown a heartbeat of its own by now and here she was right next to me, her considerable cleavage on display above the orange wet cloth at which her nipples were poking not helping any, either.

"Jack," I said, with a nod. "I'm here on business."

She arched an eyebrow, a dark, plucked thing that already had an arch. "Funny time of year to do business."

"I won't dig in till next week," I said. I didn't feel like going into my lingerie salesman routine.

"What do you sell?"

Shit.

"Things you'd look good in," I said.

"Such as?"

"Lingerie."

"Really? You don't mean that Frederick's of Hollywood type jazz?"

"Not that obvious. But sexy enough to get your husband's attention."

She looked toward the pool and the kids who weren't hers. "What makes you think I have a husband?"

"The diamond ring."

She turned to me sharply and her laugh was sharp, too. "I guess that *is* a dead giveaway....You'll be around all this coming week, then?"

"Some of it."

"Maybe we'll run into each other. I'm sometimes in the bar in the evenings."

"You'll be here a while, too?"

"Maybe. It's kind of...open-ended. Trying to work something out."

That was when I noticed that though her eyes were smiling, they had a sadness. No, that wasn't it: weariness. I'd seen that look before, just not on a good-looking woman. Guys who'd been in the jungle on one too many a tour, they got that kind of weariness in their eyes.

For a moment there, I thought maybe she'd slip her hand under the water and inside my trunks and help me out. Instead I had to wait for her to go and then do my best to get up and out of the whirlpool with my back to the other guests and those impressionable kiddies and wrap a towel around my waist and disguise my condition until I could get back to my motel room and do something about it.

About time I got a grip on myself.

Pretty soon I was climbing back into my long underwear (a real turn-on for dolls like Dorrie you picked up at a bar) and wondered how stupid it would be to indulge with this sad-eyed curvy older woman. I was on a job. Relieving tension was a good thing, when you had a job to do. But what if she somehow figured out who I was, or why I was here?

That was stupid. Nothing wrong with picking up some chick (was a thirty-five-year-old woman still a chick, I wondered?) and getting your rocks off. Might help me not go around getting raging erections in public, which is the kind of attention grabber a guy trying to stay invisible generally tries to avoid.

As I reflected on the little whirlpool mini-encounter, I realized the redhead probably hadn't been hitting on me or anything, just indulging in some gentle flirting, maybe checking to make sure she still had what it takes to get a younger guy's attention.

And how had I reacted? I'd gone off on another wild-ass mental scenario, this time involving some housewife from Who-the-Fuck-Cares Junction, probably because the professor was getting some and I wasn't.

Shit, I should cut the old boy some slack. Why shouldn't he enjoy himself a little in his last days? I was young. I had plenty of time ahead of me to get my ashes hauled. Give the dead guy a break.

Before long I was back at my window in the split-level, in my corduroy jacket over my clothes and long johns under them, with the space heater making its electrical whine. I had another thermos of hot chocolate, and a six-pack of canned Cokes and a gourmet selection of beef jerky and Slim Jims and a package of those yellow Hostess Cupcakes with the orange frosting that they don't sell year-round.

The overcast day threw soft blue shadows on the wintry landscape. The cottage looked homey and quaint; the Corvette parked out front, already white, took on a lumpy, surrealistic look with the layering of snow. After two and a half hours, I was starting to wonder if Annette had moved in with the prof for the rest of winter break, which would make my job much harder. I would have to wait for her to leave on some errand of shopping or a doctor's appointment or whatever-the-fuck, and run across the street and get the job done with no notion of when she might be back.

Also, the lack of activity over there was numbing. I began to think I was looking at a photograph, and would squint until I could see some movement from the light wind, branches rustling, snow blowing, anything to convince me otherwise. The radio station I was listening to was on its second pass through its play list—"Spill the Wine" had come around again and, if memory served, would be followed by "War," which apparently was worth absolutely nothing, as if I needed a fucking song to tell me.

That was when the dark green Pontiac GTO rolled up in front of my split-level and I ducked down, even though from where I was sitting I probably couldn't be seen, anyway. Like a kid peeking over a fence, checking if the coast was clear before sneaking into a ball game, I edged my eyes up to where I could see who the hell my visitor was.

Nobody was getting out of the GTO, which was a nice set of wheels, by the way. I could make out a figure with brown hair (Beatles '64 length), mutton chops and a trim mustache behind the wheel, just sitting there with the motor going and the windows up. No snow was on the car, either, so he'd either cleaned it off or had just arrived from enough of a drive to completely melt it off.

He was in a tan cowhide jacket with fleece lining. Had sunglasses on, even though the sun was M.I.A. He began pounding on the steering wheel with the heel of a hand. And "War" was indeed playing on my radio and this guy was keeping time to it, which kind of freaked me out.

Then I figured it was either a coincidence or he was listening to the same station. Nonetheless, I picked up the nine millimeter automatic from where it lay by my thermos of hot chocolate and I held onto it tight. I felt colder all of a sudden and leaned over and drew the space heater closer; it hummed but not in tune with "War."

When "War" ended, and "Get Ready" began, the guy was still sitting there. He wasn't watching my split-level, that was for sure. His eyes hadn't turned my way even once, not a casual quick check on his surroundings. He was glued to the cobblestone cottage.

This guy was staking out the same fucking house as me! Not very damn subtly, I grant you, though his ass-hanging-out method did validate my own more careful approach. As I resumed my normal position at the window—normal except for the gun being in my hand and resting in my lap—I frowned at the mustached kid (and that's what he was, a kid, even younger than me) who was suddenly smack dab in the middle of my surveillance.

Okay, I thought, *this is* really *getting fucked up.*

If this was what my new career was going to be like, I might want to consider signing on with Air America instead: there was always room for another mercenary in this shithole of a world.

Here's the thing: this little prick in sunglasses, with a cool ride that made my Opel GT back home look like a kiddy car, did not match up with any of the surveillance info the Broker had given me. I had a list of names and descriptions that included four guys who were staying in Iowa City over winter break, who the prof was the advisor of or some shit, and who might stop by his pad for an hour or two of legitimate college work, as opposed to coeds stopping by to polish his professorial knob. I had cars and license plates on this quartet (none of whom had shown as yet) and addresses and even goddamn phone numbers, like that would come in handy.

"Hi. My name's Quarry. I'm in town to blow your favorite professor's brains out. Can you tell me whether you're planning to stop by his place this afternoon, so I can pick a time when I wouldn't have to spray your fucking brains against the wall, too? Thanks!"

So who the hell was this little bastard?

"Let It Be" was on the radio now, doing its endless thing; apparently the DJ had to take a dump. I watched the GTO. Here I was, supposedly keeping an eye on the cobblestone cottage, and now I had this green machine on my mind. Further, he was seated in front of my split-level, inadvertently calling attention to me, or anyway my post.

The front door of the cottage opened.

For a moment, I thought the brunette was finally leaving, and doing so coincidental to the GTO's arrival; but I'd been right before, when I figured the sleek Pontiac on this quiet street would attract attention. She appeared on the porch, breath pluming, holding her arms to herself in the cold—she did not have the fur-collar coat on, just a black sweater and the same black-and-white geometric-pattern bell bottoms as yesterday.

She trotted down the sidewalk, long legs pumping, and was heading across the street as the kid in the GTO got out, his breath pluming, too. He was of medium height and on the slight side.

"*Tom!*" Her teeth were bared and her eyes large. She loomed, at least an inch taller than the kid. "What the hell do you think you're *doing*?"

"Then it's true?"

She stood there, hugging her arms to her body, shivering. "Then what is true?"

"You *are* shacked with that creep!"

Even at this distance, from the meager crack of my window, I could hear her sharp, indignant draw of breath.

"Professor Byron is my advisor! I *told* you I couldn't see you over break. We are working on a very, *very* important project."

"I bet you are! I just *bet* you are!"

This guy sure had some snappy responses.

She was shaking her head, the brunette locks bouncing every which way. "I *told* you. I told you he was helping me with my book. It's the most important thing in my life right now."

"More important than *me*?"

"Yes! Right now, *yes*. I don't have time to see you right now, and you know yourself things aren't the same, anyway, not with the distance between us."

He was waving his arms a little, not in a threatening way. Just desperate. "We could see each other probably twice a month, if you wanted to. If you weren't so intent on this *stupid* project of yours...."

"That's what you *think* of me, isn't it?"

"What...?"

"I'm nothing to you but your 'girl'—I'm not a serious writer doing serious work!"

I wondered if a serious writer would use the word "serious" twice in the same sentence. But what did I know about it?

Her arm went out straight from her side and she pointed toward the main drag that Country Vista bisected—the gesture of a parent ordering a child to its room.

"*Go*, Tom! Go back to your frat brothers. Or go home to Mommy and Daddy, I don't give a damn. Maybe you can work at the *bank* over break!"

He put his hands on her shoulders. "Annette, please—come with me. Spend the afternoon with me.

You'll freeze out here. Your teeth are chattering. Come on, baby, give me a chance. Give *us* a chance."

I wish I could tell you the radio was playing "Give Peace a Chance," but I can't. Actually, "Let It Be" was still going, though I'd turned it down very low, to hear this little soap opera.

She shook off his hands from her shoulders. "*Go!* Tommy—go! Right now. And don't bother us."

"Us?"

"We are working, K.J. and me."

"K.J." The kid shook his head. "First name basis now, you and the prof."

Actually, initials aren't really a first name, but I got his point.

"Tommy…"

"Listen, babe, I asked around about him. I talked to people."

"You don't even *go* to Iowa. How would you know?"

"I have friends. I know people. He was at Columbia two years ago, and—"

She shoved him against his car. The sound was loud enough to really carry, a substantial *whump*.

"Get the fuck out of my life," she said, teeth bared again, and she turned and strode toward the cottage.

Tom went right after her, and that was when, finally, the prof came out. He was in a beige sweater and tan chinos and sandals, but he charged right out into the winter weather and caught Tom by the arm and hauled him across the street and flung him against the car again. Byron, his dark yellow hair a straw-like tangle, had a wild-eyed look as he leaned in to Tom, whose back was to me, pushed up against the GTO.

"You are *leaving* now," Byron said, some oratory in the baritone. "Of your own volition. Otherwise, get back in your car and wait for the police to arrive, because that's the call I'm making when I get back inside, if your vehicle is still here. Do I make myself clear?"

Tom scrambled into the car and got behind the wheel and drove off in a cloud of exhaust fumes. Byron walked back and positioned himself, arms folded, about halfway up the walk and watched as his unwanted guest had to go through the humiliation of pulling into the no-name lane the split-levels were on, backing out, and turning around. Poor little bastard couldn't even make a quick getaway.

But I could.

I headed to the back of the house where I could exit unseen and scrambled like hell to get my rental Ford out of the split-level-next-door's garage. I was moving fast, damn near running, because if I didn't shake it, Tom would be long gone.

And I needed to follow Tom. He was a new player in this game and, unlike the blonde yesterday, might turn back up in the middle of things and at a very inconvenient time. If the Broker's trusty surveillance expert wasn't going to give me all the dope I needed, and I don't mean hash, I had to do the job myself.

By the time I came out of the lane and turned onto Country Vista, the professor was back in his cottage, but Tom was visible up ahead three blocks or so. I thought the kid might go tearing out of there, but instead he was crawling. We were almost to the main drag when he pulled over, and gave me a real start.

I had to go on by him and glimpsed him, hunkered over the wheel, crying.

Poor bastard.

I waited for an opening, then cut across the main drag into the parking lot of a medical clinic and waited there for the green GTO to appear at the mouth of Country Vista. Within minutes, it did, Tommy getting himself under control enough to drive, and I fell in behind him. His car had Illinois license plates; interesting. Also, a PEACE NOW bumper sticker, the O of NOW the familiar peace symbol; a second sticker said, REMEMBER KENT STATE.

They didn't make frat boys like they used to.

Before long I had followed Tom into the Iowa City business district, a ghost town on this Sunday afternoon; parking places were usually at a premium, but neither Tom nor I had trouble finding one. This was Clinton Street and the buildings of the university sprawled to my right, as I sat in my rental, and a street of bookstores, boutiques and bars was at my left. I watched Tom angle across to the Airliner, a long-in-the-tooth brick-fronted establishment whose sign bragged about its 1944 origin. Customers were sitting in a big front window eating slices of pizza and drinking beer and looking across at the snowy campus as if something were going on.

After five minutes, I cut across the barely existent

traffic and entered the bar, which didn't seem to have been remodeled since 1944, either. The pizza smell was inviting, though, and I would have taken a booth and burrowed in with a small pie if I hadn't noticed Tom sitting at the bar in his fleece-lined jacket. Most of the stools were open, so plopping down next to him and getting friendly might have been read wrong.

So I left a stool between us and ordered a beer and asked the bartender if I could eat at the bar and he said sure. I ordered a small pepperoni and, my beer not here yet, turned toward Tom and said, "I hope the pizza is as good as it smells."

Slouched over the bar, Tom gave me a "huh" look— he already had his beer, and most of it was gone—and then forced a smile and said, "It is good."

"You're from here?"

He shook his head. I was getting a better look at him now but he was just another of these semi-long-haired college kids with mustaches and fetus faces. "I go to Northwestern," he said. "Evanston?"

That explained the Illinois license plates.

I said, "I'm starting here, second semester. What's your major?"

"I'm in pre-law."

Tom wasn't unfriendly but neither was he interested, so I cut if off there. I sipped my beer, Tom ordered a second one. We did not speak again until my pizza arrived. The bartender, God bless him, placed it on the bar next to me, in front of the empty stool that separated Tom and me.

"Hey," I said to Tom. "This is more than I can handle. Help yourself to a few slices."

Tom frowned at me, then smiled. "That's nice, brother, but…I'm not that hungry."

"Come on. Why let it go to waste? Consider it a late Christmas present."

He thought about that, shrugged, and moved over a seat.

The pie was in fact excellent, a thin crust with a lot of tomato sauce and just the right amount of mozzarella and seemed to me just about the best pizza ever, although you should factor in that I'd been living on Slim Jims, beef jerky and Hostess cupcakes.

I kept the conversation casual. "You got folks in Iowa City?"

"No," he said. He was finished with his second beer and I called the bartender over and ordered us both another. Tom thanked me and said, "My girlfriend lives here."

"Really? Local gal?"

"No. Actually, she's from Chicago, too. She's a little older than me, but we've gone together since high school."

"How much older?"

He shrugged. "Just a year. But she's in grad school now. That's why she's at Iowa."

"Oh?"

"Yeah—Writers' Workshop? Really famous writers' school. Lots of big deal literary lights teach here. Kurt Vonnegut. Richard Yates. Phillip Roth."

I'd read Vonnegut.

I said, "Yeah, I know all about that. I'm going to be in the Workshop myself."

His eyebrows went up. "No kidding. Nice going— tough to get in. My girlfriend has been winning writing awards since she was in grade school."

"What's her name?"

"Annette Girard."

"Speaking of which…my name's Jack." I wiped pizza sauce off my hand and extended it to him and grinned. "Jack Harper."

"Tom Keenan," he said, and we shook.

"So," I said, "why are you sitting with some doofus in a bar, eating pizza and drinking beer, if your girl's in town?"

"She is, but…man, can I ask you something?"

"Sure."

"It's the kind of question you can only ask some doofus…some *other* doofus…in a bar." He laughed humorlessly. "Are all women untrustworthy little bitches?"

I shrugged. "Not all."

"Really?"

"Well…none that aren't come to mind." I smiled. "But you'd figure there'd have to be some of 'em out there who wouldn't cheat on your ass."

He grunted. "You *been* there, then?"

"Listen, let me tell you. I did a tour in Nam."

His eyebrows went up. "Really?"

"Yeah. And when I came home, guess where I found my honeybun?"

"In bed with a guy?"

"In bed with a guy."

We toasted beers.

"So what now, Tom? You gonna go talk sense to the little lady? Try to win her back?"

He sighed and shook his head. "Naw. She's really... really not a bad girl, Jack. She's smart and ambitious and talented and smart." He was on his fourth beer. "But her parents, her father particularly, spoiled the shit out of her. So she's used to getting her own way."

"Is she cute?"

"Cute ain't half of it! She looks like she walked out of a *Penthouse* centerspread."

Particularly on your fourth beer, when you could get the soft focus just right.

"Then," I said, "if I were you, I would forgive her lovely ass, no matter what she did to me."

He laughed. Actually laughed. "Yeah. And some day I may get her back. But right now? This prick has filled her head with all kinds of garbage."

"What prick? What kind of garbage?"

"Well, it's this goddamn professor." He sneered, shook his head. "Her fucking literary guru. Hell, he may wind up your teacher, Jack, in the Workshop!"

"Yeah? What's his name?"

"Byron. Some initials in front of that, but I forget what the fuck they are."

I was nodding. "Yeah, I know who you mean. He had a bestseller a while back, but he's sure as hell no Vonnegut."

"That's for fuckin' A sure. But she's been working

on this book, this novel…actually, she says it's a non-fiction novel—you know, like *In Cold Blood*?"

"What's it about?"

He shrugged elaborately. "I don't know. Probably her father."

"Why her father?"

He just waved that off. I was already getting more out of him than a doofus in a bar had any right.

"But this Byron asshole," Tom said, "he's an expert at this stuff. That bestseller of his, it was one of these non-fiction novel deals."

"Really."

"Yeah. Anyway, she's under his spell. But it'll only be temporary. If I go off and live my life for a while, and fuck me a few honeys back in Evanston, maybe I can forget her for now, and then, down the road a ways, we can start back up again, with a clean slate."

"The professor's just a fling?"

"Yeah, but it's *Annette* who's gettin' flung. This prof, he's a well-known horndog. I asked around about him. He's been at three colleges in six years, a dirty old man playing Mick Jagger to *lit*-rah-chure groupies."

"Your girl's just another in that long line?"

He nodded. "The bastard'll discard her like the rest of the hundred fuck-bunnies he's run through."

"Would you take her back?"

"In a goddamn heartbeat." He pushed a half-eaten slice away. "You think I'm a pussy, Jack?"

Kind of.

"No," I said. "She's just going through a phase. So then, what? You'll head back to Evanston?"

"Yeah. Or anyway to Naperville. That's where my folks live. That's also the Chicago area. But I'll crash in some motel, first. I can't drive after all this beer."

"Don't blame you. Then you'll head home tomorrow?"

"First thing."

That was good to hear.

He seemed like a nice kid. Would have been a drag having to kill him.

FOUR

By four o'clock that afternoon, I had resumed my post in the split-level, and while my space heater and my radio and my dwindling supply of 7-Eleven delicacies were waiting patiently for me, the brunette's white Corvette had finally departed.

This was good news, or anyway news, as it seemed to indicate Annette had not moved in over break with Professor Byron after all. That might have cleared a path for me to slip across the street, especially after sundown, and close the book on the supposedly famous writer, only another car was out front.

I knew whose car this was—a yellow Corvair from the early sixties, a model known to have a few deficiencies, such as leaking oil, impaling its driver on the steering column in a collision, sending noxious fumes into the interior, and occasionally blowing up. This specimen seemed pretty much in one piece, with dents here and there and twice as many anti-war and anti-Nixon bumper stickers as Tom's GTO.

This questionable ride belonged to one of the four male students from the Writers' Workshop who Professor Byron was known to advise. For just a moment I considered going over there and snuffing both of them, since they were both dead men, the prof my contracted target and his student a Corvair driver.

Around six-thirty, already dark as midnight but with a nearly full moon washing the snow an ivory-blue, the student exited—a skinny kid in a gray parka and jeans and galoshes. His nest of facial hair stuck out like a porcupine was sitting on his face. A porcupine with granny glasses on its ass. The prof stayed in the doorway and watched his charge stride toward the Corvair with the confidence of a Lafayette Escadrille pilot about to go up after the Red Baron. I figured his odds of getting home were about the same.

That left the prof alone in his cottage, and me wondering if I should spend a couple of more days updating the obviously flawed surveillance info I'd been given, before laying my ass on the line. Maybe Annette hadn't moved out—maybe she'd skedaddled to the shopping mall over on the southeast side, to kill time while Professor Loverboy dealt with a student who was presumably stopping by to deliver breathless prose and not a blowjob.

By that reasoning, the brunette might wander in right when I was fulfilling the contract. If all I had to do was pop this fucker, that might be worth the risk—I could be in and out in minutes. But I had that extra assignment of rounding up certain manuscript pages and disposing of them—that "challenge" Broker had given me, as his new boy.

An hour went by and no Annette. The radio station had cycled through its playlist for the fourth or fifth time, and "American Woman" was back on when I decided to do something more than sit on my ass. I had Annette's address, which was in Coralville, a small suburb to the west of Iowa City. I drove there.

She was on the second floor of a little modern red-brick apartment complex, six apartments up, five down, all with exterior entrances, the walkway above providing the first floor with an overhang. A laundry room on the lower level seemed to be the only shared living experience here.

The apartment facility was just a block off Coralville's busy retail and restaurant strip, an artery pumping monetary life's blood into the little suburb. And I was able to park in the lot of a Sambo's restaurant on the corner, the Maverick nosed in against the cement-block six-foot wall that separated the restaurant from its residential next-door neighbor, but with a clear view of Annette's digs. She was on the second floor, apartment 204, with her white Corvette parked in a specified spot in the complex's tiny parking lot.

The curtained windows of her apartment glowed yellow. She was in there, maybe writing. She had to produce material for her advisor to advise her over, right? For maybe an hour, I sat watching those windows, figuring if she stayed in her nest until, say, midnight, she wasn't likely to go back out and rejoin the prof.

This wasn't scientific. I was learning on the job, which is to say making it up as I went along. But I was giving serious thought to making tonight the night—drive back to my split-level and go over to the cobblestone cottage and get this the fuck over with. The longer I hung around, it seemed, the more wild cards were getting played. In a game like that, you either play what's dealt you and hope for the best, or you get the hell away from the table.

And what would the Broker say if I bailed on my very first contract? Not only would I be a disappointment to my new employer, I'd be an instant loose end. This wasn't the kind of job, wasn't the kind of business, where you can apply, get a position, discover you're not right for it, shake hands with the boss and say thanks anyway and go along your merry way, until the next position came along. No. I knew the Broker was a middleman in the murder business, and that was dangerous information to possess, in and of itself. On top of that, I knew about the Concort Inn and could extrapolate that the Quad Cities was Broker's base of operations.

If I didn't want to go through with this, I would have to disappear and leave behind my A-frame on the lake and money in the bank and still risk getting shot to shit by some asshole sent by the Broker.

Amway and the Jehovah's Witnesses were looking better all the time.

I'd been watching maybe another half hour when she came out of her apartment and trotted down the central staircase, a big white purse on a strap over her shoulder. Again she was in the white leather coat with the white fur collar; her bell bottoms were dark blue with black polka dots that didn't show till she'd crossed the street and walked right past where I was parked.

I watched her go into the Sambo's.

What the hell. I went in after her. I hadn't eaten since the pizza at the Airliner.

The restaurant had a motif based on the old children's book about little black Sambo chasing tigers around a tree until they turned into butter, which must have seemed like a fun concept for a chain of pancake houses until Black Power came along. The Sambo kid on the menus and in decorative art in this aggressively bright orange-and-white restaurant was not black, rather some vague turbaned Oriental type, like that wouldn't offend somebody in a college town like Iowa City.

The place was damn near empty, Sunday night during break, a few families in booths and a couple of truck drivers at the endless counter, with the young waiters and waitresses in their orange outfits and caps stricken with that hollow expression that says, *How did my life bottom out so soon?*

I took a counter seat and ordered some eggs and pancakes and sausage and iced tea. I was able from here to see Annette, seated by herself in a corner booth, reading a book whose title was *Armies of the Night*; I wasn't actually seated close enough to see that, but I'd picked up on it when I walked past her.

Her coat was off—the heat was going at a pretty good clip here in the tropical world of Sambo's—and she had on a black sweater that made the polka dots on the purple slacks stand out more; her smallish breasts under the sweater were doing a swell job, considering. She wasn't eating anything, at least not yet, just working on a cup of black coffee.

She seemed fairly engrossed in the book. I had my eggs, sausage and pancakes, "tiger butter" and all, and decided to take a risk. Maybe it was the sugar rush.

On my way to the counter to pay my bill, I stopped at her booth and asked, "How is that?"

She glanced up from her paperback, not at all irritated by the interruption, and said in a nice throaty alto, "Do you like Norman Mailer?"

"I've only read *Naked and the Dead*," I said, which was true. I read it in high school back when I thought war sounded like a heroic thing for a kid to get involved in. Mailer's opinion had been different, and now so was mine, although he hadn't had anything to do with it.

"Well, he's a completely out of control egotist," she said. "Or perhaps I should say ego-*ist*."

Was there a difference? Not if you hadn't been to college there wasn't.

She was saying, "But he may be onto something here—referring to himself in the third person and all."

I nodded toward the book in her scarlet-nailed hands. "Isn't that non-fiction? Something about the march on the Pentagon?"

"Yes. But it's a non-fiction *novel*, or at least it's trying to be. I don't know if he's really successful here, but it's interesting to see him try. I really think this is the future."

"Yeah. Of what?"

She beamed at me in a winning combination of embarrassment and confidence. "Of the novel. Of journalism. I don't know really, but *something* new."

"Does sound interesting."

I smiled and nodded, and she smiled and nodded

back and returned to her book, and I went on outside
and climbed into the Maverick and got the heat going.

No way to know how long Mailer's book and Sambo's
coffee would hold her interest; no way to know if she'd
be heading back to her place or the prof's cottage,
after. I could sit here and wait and watch to see when
she emerged, five minutes or two hours from now, but
if she noticed me, that would be bad. That was the
downside of getting friendly with my target's best girl.
I couldn't think of an upside, incidentally. I just kind of
liked her looks.

Less than half an hour later I was back at the old
stand. The space heater was doing fine and in fact was
making me a little sleepy; well, the space heater and
those pancakes—blame the tiger butter. A car be-
longing to another of those male Writers' Workshop
students was parked in front of the cobblestone pad,
meaning a legit advisory session was again under way.

This meant Annette might be staying away just until these meetings were over. Another half an hour
dragged by and I was sipping some cocoa from the
thermos lid-cup when I heard a crinkling sound. Now
this new house had plastic down on the floors, but I
had rolled the living room sheet back to give me a nice
space by and around the window where I could sit on
carpet and not on cold crinkly plastic. I mention this
because the plastic could also serve as an early warning
system, alerting me to somebody else moving through
this house.

Of course, I would have to have been fully awake
and not trying to maintain surveillance with my head

up my ass, and when I removed my head from that ori-
fice and turned, I was facing a guy with a gun. Which is
to say, I wasn't facing him with my gun, he was facing
me with *his*, a little .38 Police Special with a snub nose,
a dinky nothing that could kill you deader than Jimi
and Janis.

He was short and dark and pudgy with Nixon jowls
and tiny dark eyes and an awful bulb of a nose. He had
no hat on a mostly bald noggin, though the hair he did
have was longish, enough so that he had sideburns, not
quite mutton chops but close. He was in a tan trench-
coat that had a lumpiness indicating it was heavily
lined; and brown slacks and brown rubber-soled shoes.

He was grinning, not a very wide grin, but a toothy
Bucky Beaver thing that gave him a hint of childish
glee. Whoever he was, he figured he'd really put one
over on me.

Which he had.

"Just take it easy, kid," he said. His voice was a fairly
squeaky tenor, not at all impressive, except for be-
longing to a guy with a gun.

The nine millimeter was in my waistband but my
corduroy jacket was zipped. Maybe I could slip my
hand up and under and get at the weapon; and maybe
not. Probably not.

"Why don't you come over here, kid," he said, and
motioned with the .38. "Get away from the windows."

"I'm okay where I am."

"No, really, you aren't. I'm not going to shoot you."

"Then put the gun down."

"Not till we're better acquainted. I think we might

work for the same team…well, not the same team. But maybe affiliated teams, you know?"

I didn't say anything, because I *didn't* know. I did get to my feet and I walked over to the half of the living room still covered in plastic, my footsteps crinkling it this time. I faced him but kept my distance, maybe four feet.

"Listen, kid," he said, regret in his voice but the Bucky Beaver grin still going, "I gotta pat you down."

"I don't think that's a good idea."

His eyes got hard and the grin vanished; his mouth was a puckery thing in the five o'clock-shadowed face, an anus that wandered off course. "You put your hands up, kid, and stand for a frisk. Be a good boy. I been at this longer than you. I got *ties* older than you."

That I believed.

I put my hands up. I was ready to bring them down on him, but he was experienced, I'll give him that. When he got close, he shoved the snout of the revolver in my side and with his free hand unzipped my coat.

"Now that's a weapon," he said admiringly of the nine millimeter in my waistband. He plucked the gun like a metal flower and dropped it in a trenchcoat pocket and backed up a couple steps.

Was I dead?

"Let me guess," he said genially. "You're working for the father."

"Am I?"

His somewhat Neanderthal brow wrinkled. "Don't answer questions with questions. It's annoying."

"Is it?"

The bucktooth grin again. "You have a sense of humor. That's good. Because people with senses of humor, they have a certain love of life. What is it the French say?"

"*Merde*?"

"*Joie de vivre.* And people with a love of life don't take stupid chances, particularly when they don't have to. I don't wanna kill you, kid. Really I don't. It would be a real pain in my keister, and neither would I want to piss off the girl's father."

"Who would?"

He chuckled. "You know, you're pretty good. I didn't spot you till today. How many days you been here?"

"This is the second."

"Well, I've been on the job for three days. I'm in the split-level house across the way. I saw you take your car out earlier this evening. That's maybe not a good idea in the daylight."

"You may be right."

"Who do you think I'm working for?"

"Not the girl's father." That's all I could think of to say—my information was limited.

"No," he said, shaking his head in agreement, "not the girl's father, which is a pity."

"Is it?"

His tiny glittery eyes tightened. His nose was really ugly, with veins and blackheads and whiteheads in the crevices. And those beaver teeth were yellow, probably from smoking, because he stank of it. Death is never pretty, but did I really have to get killed by somebody this unpleasant?

He moved just a little closer. The gun-in-hand was angled away just a shade, to make me feel less threatened, I guess, and more like we were pals. Or anyway, business associates. Affiliated teams and all.

"The wife has money," he said confidentially. "I mean, the prof has done fairly well, hasn't he? Movie sale on that book of his, a big advance for this opus he's knocking out now."

So he was working for the professor's wife—that made sense: a philandering husband can attract the likes of this bucktoothed frog.

"You're a private eye," I said.

He reared back with a blink and a grin. "Yeah, of course I'm a PI. Like *you* are. That is, unless you're just one of daddy's regular helpers, which you don't look like in the least. Anyway, he's all tied up with that nigger problem, ain't he?"

"Yeah. Fuckin' spooks." What the hell was he talking about?

He sighed, shook his head. "You know, those Italians think Chicago is their birthright, and when a bunch of uppity spades start moving in on the dope business, things can get hairy."

"That's for sure."

"But if we know one thing about these Outfit wops, it's that they are rolling in dough. *Illegal* dough, sure, but dough don't know where it comes from."

"Right."

"Like I said, the wife has money. But the girl's father has *real* money."

"No argument."

He moved his weight from one brown shoe to the other. "Hey. This is awkward. I mean…we're gonna be friends, kid. What's your name?"

"Jack."

"And I'm Charlie."

"Pleasure to meet you, Charlie." I extended my hand but he didn't take it—his right hand was busy pointing a gun at me, after all. "What kind of friendship are we going to have?"

"The business kind. Let's go out in the kitchen and sit down and make this nice and friendly and non-hostile, shall we?"

"Sure. After you."

He horse-laughed, flecking my face with spittle. "Naw, Jack, I think *you'll* lead the way. Sense of humor. Kid's got a sense of humor.…"

The kitchen, a modern, spacious white-and-gray affair, had no plastic on the floor, just linoleum. A breakfast nook with a little table in a booth right out of a restaurant was off to one side, with a window that let in moonlight. He motioned me in and then slid in and sat across from me, his hand with the .38 on the table, casual but ready, like a fork in his fist as he anticipated a meal.

"Now, let's think about this," he said in that genial if squeaky tenor. "We have clients with similar interests, right? Both of them want that cheating prick of a professor hung out to dry by his gonads."

"Agreed."

His round head tilted. "But there are places where we overlap, our interests…and places where we don't overlap. Would you agree on that point, too?"

"I may not be following you."

He shrugged. Frowned, dark little pellet eyes narrowing. "My client, the wife, wants evidence on this horny asshole, so she can divorce his unfaithful ass and get as much of his loot as possible."

"Oh…kay."

With his free hand, he gestured grandiosely. "And I have photos that demonstrate this fact—some that catch him naked as a jaybird…with females the same buck nekkid way."

"You didn't get that from sitting across the street. Through a window, huh? Up close and personal?"

"Yeah—I got him through his study window and his bedroom, too." He leaned across a little. "You know, this guy likes to gets blown more than he wants to get fucked; he likes to sit in his chair in that study and have those sweet young things worship his cock."

"Better than no religion at all, I guess."

He snorted his laugh and I backed up a little, in hopes of avoiding spittle; no such luck. "You're a funny kid, Jack. That sense of humor. I just knew we were gonna be tight."

"So you have photos of Annette and Byron."

He leaned back; the grin widened again, his pride palpable. "Damn straight. But I also got photos of him and a little blonde. Which is where things get interesting."

I frowned. "You mean, that girl Alice, who tore the professor a new asshole yesterday?"

"Yeah. He was banging her the morning before. Or she was blowing him or whatever. Anyway, she was in there with him, and they kissed in the doorway for about a month, before she left in her little car, happy as a clam. And then that afternoon, the brunette showed."

"This is the day before yesterday?"

"Yeah."

"Did she stay the night, Annette?"

"No. But she did *last* night." He smiled cannily. "You knew that, though."

"Yeah. Just trying to get a pattern down." I shook my head. "It's Grand Central Station around here."

He leaned in with his yellow grin. "But that's a *good* thing, Jack. See, we can serve both our masters and still make some real money."

"How?"

He shrugged elaborately. "Your boss wants to confirm that the prof is banging his daughter. You've pretty much accomplished that by now, so I figure before long? You, or one or more of the Chicago bent-nose boys, will come lean on the prof and teach *him*, for a change."

"You mean kill him?"

"No! No, I don't think so." He laughed heartily, genuinely amused. "I'm not supposed to think you're a *hit* man, Jack! Please. Nice clean-cut kid like you— you really fit in around here, which is great. I could use somebody like you, your age, able to blend with these hippie shits."

"Thank you."

"Naw, the girl's father will put the fear of God into that horny bastard, and the prof will stay away from daddy's little girl in future, out of fear of something worse happening."

I shifted in the booth. "Okay. Let's say you're right. Let's say you've figured this out perfectly. Where do our interests converge, Charlie? Where's money to be made for you and me?"

The grin widened and the Nixon jowls turned into chipmunk cheeks. "If I give my pictures of daddy's little girl going down on the Prof to my client...Mrs. Prof? Of sweet Annette riding Byron's pecker like a rodeo queen? Then those photos could find their way into divorce court, and lots of embarrassment, the tabloid variety, could ensue."

"Okay. I can see that."

With the hand not holding the gun, Charlie held up a finger, as if he'd just had a brilliant idea, though he'd obviously been working on this a while. "*But*—I also have pictures of the prof with the little blonde, every *bit* as damning. These I could give to my client. Then I will sell the pictures of Annette and the prof, and the negatives, no tricks, none whatsoever, to her father. We don't need the Annette shots to make the divorce case. Your client is happy. My client is happy. We are happy. What do you say, Jack?"

"It makes sense. You have a figure in mind?"

His eyebrows lifted. "What do you think the market will bear? I mean, this is not the kind of person you want to piss off, the girl's father."

I lifted my eyebrows. "No he isn't." I leaned forward conspiratorially. "Could you live with ten grand?"

He thought about that, then demonstrated his math skills out loud: "Half of ten, five for me, five for you?"

I shook my head. "No—I think ten apiece is possible. Without seeming too greedy and getting our asses in a sling."

The tiny eyes glittered. "Cool! We have a deal then?"

I grinned at him. "We have a deal."

Again I held my hand out for him to shake. This time he put the .38 on the table and extended his hand and I picked the gun up and shot him between the eyes, right above that disgusting nose.

After the sharp crack of the gunshot, I said, "Goodbye, Charlie...or as the French say, *adieu*."

Knowing how much he appreciated my sense of humor.

But he didn't hear me, too busy flopping onto the tabletop, his forehead making a dull *thump* as he left on the wall behind him a nice splash of color in this drab kitchen.

FIVE

I had things to do, and Charlie wasn't going anywhere, slumped as he was at the breakfast nook tabletop, like a school kid napping at his desk. In his right trench-coat pocket I removed not only my nine millimeter but his car keys and also, on a separate little ring, three keys—each had tiny strips of masking tape with black-marker lettering that identified one as FRONT, another as BASEMENT and the other, which was somewhat smaller, as PATIO.

His gun I dropped into my right-hand corduroy jacket pocket, and I slipped out the back way into the cold, my feet crunching on snow that had turned crispy with ice. My nine millimeter was back in my waistband and I figured anything that came up, Charlie's .38 would do nicely, a gun after all traceable to him. I went into the garage not to get my car, but to remove a flashlight from my glove compartment; the flash I dropped in my other coat pocket, and then I returned to the great out of doors.

Perhaps I was overcautious, but I moved along the back yards of the half dozen split-levels on my side of the unlived-on lane. No street lamps were up yet on the nameless street but that full moon illuminated the landscape, so I felt I should take a roundabout route to the split-level opposite mine, where Charlie said he'd been camped out. He had not mentioned working with anyone (other than me, had I gone along with him), but I saw no reason to trust a sleazy little character who would sell out, or anyway compromise, his own client. A round-the-clock surveillance, if that's what Charlie had been up to, might mean a second PI in that other split-level.

Of course, they might be trading shifts, with Charlie alone with his partner due to show up any time—assuming I wasn't just imagining this partner. At any rate, a look inside that house might tell me if Charlie had or had not been working alone.

So I went all the way down to the end of the lane and beyond into a wooded area, through which I cut just a little ways to come up through the back yards of the other half dozen split-levels. The snow was crunchy back here, too, but I moved very slowly and carefully; on the other hand, if the interior of Charlie's split-level had that same plastic on the floor, I might wind up fucked.

The back yard of the corner split-level, the doppel-ganger of mine, rose up at the left to a patio area and dropped at the right to accommodate a driveway and allow entry to the basement and garage. One of these keys apparently opened the glass doors onto the patio. These would open onto a family room, where plastic on the floor would almost certainly await.

The basement door seemed my best option. Much as I didn't relish entering into darkness and then going up the stairs and opening a door onto God knew what (or I should say God knew who), going in the patio way and snap-crackle-popping across a covered floor held even less appeal.

Of course when I said I'd be coming up from the basement into God knows what, that was an exaggeration, even an inaccuracy, because I knew darn well the kitchen—the only room in my split-level where the floor hadn't been covered with protective plastic— would be waiting. Of course, so could Charlie's partner, should he happen to exist.

So I used the basement key and went on into darkness and, remembering the layout across the street, made my way fairly easily to the stairs. I slipped out of my boots and went up in my stocking feet. At the top I turned the knob as slowly as I could, creating only the faintest click, and pushed the door open onto a darkened kitchen.

My night vision was good. Nobody was in the kitchen, unless you counted me. No lights seemed to be on in the house, which had been the case across the street, as well. But as I moved cautiously toward the expansive living room beyond the kitchen, I heard a soft, faint voice and froze.

Despite the low volume, the voice was sonorous, commanding and familiar.

It should be: it belonged to Ben Cartwright, or that is, Lorne Greene. The "Bonanza" TV theme kicked in as a television, in the living room, went to commercial—a little portable on the floor over by the window that faced Country Vista, with a view on a certain cobblestone cottage. The lighthouse beam of the tiny television illuminated the living room somewhat, creating light and shadow, and told me there were indeed some differences between my quarters and the late Charlie's.

First of all, no plastic covered the carpeted floor. Second, and most surprising, the place was furnished; no one was living here yet, no one was living in any of these split-levels except me (and the late Charlie), and yet new furniture smell joined the paint and plaster and antiseptic odors, the blocky shapes of undistinguished contemporary furnishings, right out of a Sears catalog, revealed by the TV's cathode rays.

The furnishing was fairly sparse, however, and I had little trouble maneuvering. No sign of Charlie's partner, who was starting to feel nonexistent to me. Near that floor-positioned TV, where Ben and Little Joe and Hoss were currently having an intense if barely audible conversation on horseback, Charlie had a fucking La-Z-Boy pulled over to where in my parallel world I'd been leaning against a sleeping bag. An open package of Ruffles Potato Chips was propped against the chair, and Budweiser cans were littered on the floor. The new house smells were tainted by cigarette smoke and an ashtray with eight or ten butts was on an end table he'd pulled around on the right side of the recliner.

Room by room, level by level, I searched the house. I entered doorways low, .38 in my right hand, flash in my left, sweeping the rooms with frantic slashes of light, like Zorro making one Z after another, and revealing nothing except a fully, blandly furnished house that showed no signs of humans living here.

No humans, that is, except Charlie, who had actually been sleeping on the premises. The master bedroom had a queen-size with quilt and blankets and sheets, and Charlie had tucked himself in for the nights he'd been here, really making himself at home.

And yet nobody lived here, that was for sure. No family pictures, no clothing in closets, none of the signs of life except for Charlie's food in the refrigerator, which ran to beer and cold sandwiches. A house in this price range wouldn't be sold furnished, would it?

Then it came to me: Charlie, the lucky stiff, had selected the development's model home! This struck me as foolish and even dangerous, since people might eventually come around. But maybe Charlie had known that the model home wouldn't be open for inspection for a time, making his squatting feasible. The Broker had known that I could safely camp out across the way, hadn't he? And obviously Charlie had his own reliable intel.

I spent quite a while in that house, maybe an hour. I found Charlie's camera, a high-end Nikon with a telephoto zoom attachment, and half a dozen rolls of undeveloped film, which was a nice catch. No other weapons presented themselves, not even a box of shells. I looked for a notebook and didn't find one. That was a disappointment.

I thought about wiping the house down of Charlie's fingerprints, but I couldn't convince myself it was necessary. What would the owners of the model home find? Signs that some asshole had moved in for a few days. I did take a few things with me, the kind of things an ambitious homeless guy taking advantage of an empty house wouldn't leave behind: Charlie's personal items, toiletries, changes of clothes, and skin mags, all stuffed in a little duffel bag, and that portable TV, which I thought might be nice to have.

You could access the garage through the basement, which I did (after I got my boots back on), and I put Charlie's duffel bag in his car's trunk, where I had a nice piece of luck: I found a fresh roll of electrical tape among some tools of the road. I dropped this in the same pocket as my flashlight. The little TV I rested on the rider's side seat. On an otherwise empty workbench, I found a garage door opener that made my life easier and soon I'd moved Charlie's car—a light-green Chevelle—over into the driveway of the split-level (right behind mine) whose garage was where I parked the rental Ford while on stakeout.

Back in my own digs again, I got out of my corduroy coat because I was working up a sweat, despite the cold, and tossed it onto my side of the breakfast nook. The splash of gore on the wall behind where Charlie slumped needed cleaning up, but I'd have to stop and buy paper towels and spray bottles and so on, and that just wasn't a priority. Right now I wasn't even sure I'd be in this house again, once I'd left to dispose of Charlie. That would be up to the Broker.

I did have a pocket knife on me, and that allowed me to cut just the right size sheet of plastic from the floor to roll Charlie up in. Some blood and stuff got on the kitchen linoleum, but if I did come back, that would spruce up easy enough. Charlie was awkward and heavy and he smelled bad—and I don't just mean the cigarette smoke on him and his clothes, that would have been a relief compared to the stink of shit from the bastard evacuating himself when he died. Shouldn't be critical—he couldn't help it.

He made a nice fat plastic cocoon when I was done, and I used the entire spool of electrical tape to make it happen. The fucker was literal dead weight, though, and back in my cord jacket again, I had to drag him out of there like a dog pulling a sled. The plastic mummy slid over the top of the frozen snow, and the slope down to the driveway next door was steep enough that Charlie almost got away from me. That might sound funny to you, me chasing a corpse across a bunch of snowy yards in the moonlight, but the idea of it sure didn't make me smile.

I managed to maintain control over my plastic-wrapped charge, and before long I was down in that driveway, popping the trunk and hauling him up and in. It took some doing, but rigor hadn't set in yet and Charlie was pretty pliable.

The interior of the Chevelle needed fumigation, but that was a luxury I couldn't afford; but let me tell you, chain-smoker Charlie was lucky he hadn't died of cancer. Plus, he was a slob—the front and back seat floors littered with crushed sacks and drink cups from McDonald's and Dairy Queen, with the back seat a kind of reading room, and not the *Christian Science Monitor* variety, either: boxing magazines, the *National Enquirer* and the *Globe*, men's magazines like *Stag* and *Male*, with guys fighting wild animals on some covers and sexy female Gestapo agents torturing bare-chested he-men on others. Also a few more skin books, notably *Dapper* and *Follies*, where the cover models looked like the mothers of your high school pals only in pasties and not aprons.

My karma had caught up with me—I'd killed the fucker, and now was condemned to drive his car. I backed out, drove the fraction of a block to the stop sign at Country Vista and turned left, going past the cobblestone cottage, whose resident seemed suddenly very low on my "to do" list, and made my way to the nearest pay phone, which was at a Standard Station on Dubuque Street.

I called the emergency number and, to his credit, the Broker himself answered it, on the second ring.

"We have a problem," I said.

"Oh dear."

"We need to meet."

"When?"

"Now."

"Right now?"

"Right now."

"That would be most inconvenient."

"I'm already driving a car that has something inconvenient in its trunk."

"Well, good heavens."

"Yeah, that pretty much sums it up."

"Do I need to bring someone with me?"

"Let's put it this way—I'll be driving a car that I'll have to leave behind. And I'll need a ride somewhere."

"Somewhere?"

"Where that somewhere is will be up to you."

"Oh. So this is a serious wrinkle."

"It's fucking pruney."

"All right. Understood. I have someone who can help us."

"Peachy."

"Where shall we meet?"

"Pick an all-night truckstop on the Interstate, why don't you? Between where I am and where you are."

"Fine. Drive east, toward the Quad Cities. Exit at Moscow. Look for the dinosaur."

"Moscow? Dinosaur?"

"It's one of those Sinclair gas station dinosaurs—at the Moscow, Iowa, exit."

"If you say so."

"When will you be leaving?"

"Now."

"All right—go ahead. I can organize my end quickly and you have just a little farther to go."

"I'll say."

I hung up.

When I started out, it was close to eleven. Interstate 80 was mostly big fucking trucks and me. I rolled along at seventy and might have found the ivory-cast winter landscape, with its gentle rolling terrain, serenely soothing if the tobacco smell in the car, which cracking the window didn't seem to help, wasn't damn near choking me. Charlie *would* have his revenge....

And then one of those big fucking trucks I mentioned would come along and, ten four good buddy, about blow my ass off the highway. Christ, I was almost glad to see first one and then another pulled over by the cops, or as glad as a guy with a plastic-wrapped stiff in his trunk can be to see the cops.

Charlie had some eight-tracks but it was all shit—country *and* western—and his radio seemed intent on pulling in Holy Roller preachers ("This is Garner Ted Armstrong, saying…"), additional hillbilly music ("Hello, Darlin' "), and really wretched rock stations (if "ABC" by the Jackson Five and "I Think I Love You" by the Partridge Family could be considered rock). Somewhere Charlie was laughing his ass off at me, although not in the trunk—he was nice and quiet back there.

Right alongside the Interstate, the green dinosaur loomed from in front of a Sinclair station truckstop, and I now knew the Broker's instructions hadn't been a hallucination on either of our parts. I took the Moscow exit and pulled in to a graveled parking lot filled with bigger, modern day dinosaurs, the semi variety; truckers not taking a nap in their rigs were inside having coffee and cholesterol. The Chevelle I left in a front space in front of God and everybody, and strolled into a brightly lit, wholesome-looking restaurant with a long counter.

I found a window booth, from which I ordered an iced tea, cheeseburger and fries. My waitress was a thousand years old, but was efficient for her age, and I enjoyed my meal while I waited for the Broker to show.

When he came in about fifteen minutes later, he

didn't look any more out of place than Rex Harrison at a 4-H meeting. His tan camel's hair topcoat probably cost as much as every trucker at the counter's red-and-plaid jacket put together, and his long face with the angular cheekbones and soft blue eyes and stark white hair wouldn't be any more memorable than Martians landing, should the cops ever come around asking.

With him was a guy in a denim jacket and blue jeans, hands in the pockets of the jacket, which wasn't near warm enough for winter. He was a fairly small specimen, maybe five six and of average build, but his burr haircut and dead dark eyes in a chiseled, weathered face said he was ex-military.

That didn't surprise me. I figured most of Broker's recruits came from the ranks of Uncle Sam's cast-offs. His business worked best with outsiders, trained killers who were not mob-affiliated or otherwise burdened with criminal records and backgrounds. Clean-cut all-American mercenaries.

Broker nodded at the counter and the guy in denim sat there, while his master came over, removing brown leather gloves, and giving me a smile that was only technically a smile, going up at either end but mirthless and disapproving.

He glanced at the booth fore and aft of mine, noted that they were vacant, and sat rather heavily, then slid over, creating a farting sound on the faux leather of the booth and making me smile.

I asked Broker, "Where'd you find Rumpelstiltskin?"

Broker just looked at me, his puss as blank as a pie

pan. "You might want to watch that kind of talk around Roger. He's a formidable young man. Much like yourself."

"Then maybe Roger ought to watch himself around me."

One eyebrow went up. "You seem in a surly mood."

"Maybe it's just a preemptive strike, since I figure you aren't too happy getting called out for a road trip in the middle of the night."

"And, actually, I'm not. Can you give me the rough details?"

I didn't respond to that, instead asking, "Who's going to drive me back? That's assuming you want me to *go* back."

He frowned. "I presume I will drive you, since you indicated the car you're in may…may require some clean-up."

"Ah. That's where Roger comes in."

"Correct."

I wiped a fry through the glistening red of watered-down ketchup. "I had to eliminate a business rival."

He frowned. "I see. And you feel it's best you give me the details on the ride back, rather than here in public?"

"Yeah. Not many people in this lovable greasy spoon, granted, but just the two of us in your car would be better. I gotta warn you, though. I smell like shit."

"Is that right?"

I nodded. "The car I drove belongs to that business rival I mentioned. He damn near smoked himself to death. Damn near. And now I got that foul stench in my clothes."

The Broker folded his hands prayerfully. "Pity. Did you get any identification from this rival?"

"Yeah. If you let me drive your car, I can give you that stuff and you can go over it."

He nodded crisply.

The thousand-year-old waitress came over and Broker ordered a coffee to go. She stared at him for a moment, as if she were hoping he were an apparition that might disappear and remove the need of carrying out so difficult a task, but Broker didn't disappear, so she did.

He asked, "Unavoidable, this elimination?"

"No. I needed practice."

"There's no need for sarcasm."

"Ever see *A Night at the Opera*?"

"What, the Marx Brothers? Of course I have. Why?"

I dragged another fry through red. "Remember the stateroom scene? Every member of the cast piling into a little cabin on that steamship? Well, that's this as-signment. Crawling with names and faces that weren't in that surveillance report. That's why I say you may not want me to go back there."

He sighed and shook his head. "You *have* to. This is a key client."

"From Chicago, right?"

He blanched. "How do you know that?"

"When people talk to me, I pay attention."

The Broker said nothing. His spooky blue eyes were half-lidded. He slid out of the booth, went over and tapped the denim midget on the shoulder, and he and Roger came over. Broker slid back into the booth and Roger sat next to him.

Broker said, "Quietly tell Roger what to expect."

I considered telling Roger that what he could expect was a life of getting turned away at various amusement park rides for not meeting the height requirement. But I thought better of it.

"Hi, Roger." I threw Charlie's car keys onto the booth's tabletop. Then I nodded out the window at the car parked just beyond where we sat. "You can expect to find a dead man in the trunk of that green Chevelle. Pre-wrapped in plastic, like a picnic sandwich."

Roger said, "Anything else?"

"A duffel bag of his shit. There's some skin magazines in the back seat you can help yourself to. My suggestion? Get rid of everything—the whole damn car."

Roger turned toward the Broker.

Broker said, "I concur."

Roger nodded.

Then Charlie's new chauffeur exited the booth and stopped by the counter where he'd been in the middle of his own cheeseburger and fries, and requested of the thousand-year-old waitress a to-go sack, and got back a Lot's Wife look but eventual cooperation.

By the time the Broker had paid our check, Roger and Charlie and the Chevelle were gone. We stepped into the cold air and the Broker pulled on his leather gloves. I didn't have to be told which ride was the Broker's—that silver Cadillac Fleetwood Eldorado.

I'd never been inside one before, let alone sat behind the wheel. But Broker entrusted it to me.

God, it was all leather and padded dashboard with a cassette player and still had the new car smell, and no tobacco stench at all. I felt like I was sitting in a penthouse, not a car. But I hid my reaction from Broker, who I handed Charlie's wallet.

I drove toward Iowa City, keeping it at seventy, and filled Broker in on what had happened, including Charlie's elliptical references to the girl's father and his not so-elliptical references to the professor's wife.

"He was an untrustworthy man," the Broker said of Charlie. "You made the right decision."

"But it's collateral damage."

"Ah, and you don't like collateral damage."

"No, I don't, but this guy was a sleazy prick, so I'm over it. But do we need to pull out? Scrap the contract? We have all kinds of players in this that your surveillance guy didn't pick up on."

"True. But this is a vital contract."

"Right. Because that brunette's father is a Chicago Outfit guy."

Broker didn't like hearing me say that.

"And," I went on, "he wants the prof snuffed because he doesn't like daddy's little girl taking entrance exams from a faculty member's member."

He sighed heavily. "Something like that. The 'why' is not your concern. It's not even *my* concern."

"When assholes like Charlie come waltzing into my life…into *our* life…it is. So, then, I stay?"

"You stay. But get this thing done."

"Look, Broker." My eyes were on the ivory world we were gliding through. "Bumping off a Charlie Who's-it is one thing. Putting that brunette at risk is another."

He straightened as much as his seat belt would allow. "Well, under no circumstances take *her* out. My God, she's the client's daughter."

"Even if she wanders in on me in the process?"

"Wear a ski mask if you have to."

"Oh, this just gets classier."

"Quarry...there's nothing classy about murder."

"Says the guy in the camel's hair coat with the Fleetwood Caddy."

He didn't have anything to say to that.

Then the Broker turned on a little light on his side of the vast vehicle and went through all that I.D. I'd handed over.

"You've looked at this," he said.

"Yeah. Like I said, he was a PI."

Broker nodded and went through the credit cards and various papers tucked in with the cash in the fold.

"What does this mean?" he asked, reading aloud from a slip of paper, " 'We'll meet on Monday night at the Holiday Inn lounge. 7 p.m. D.B.' "

I shrugged. "Could be this case—could be something else of Charlie's, something old."

He frowned at me. "Is that what you think?"

"It's possible that 'B' stands for 'Byron,' and that this note is from Charlie's client."

"The wife."

"The wife."

I glanced over at the Broker and his expression was stricken.

"That means," he said, "we could have the professor's *wife* added to your stateroom scene."

"If that memo does mean what I speculated it might, yes. And of course it might not."

"Christ. Hell."

"So then we *do* pull out?"

"Can you think of another alternative? I would be grateful, Quarry, if you could."

I shrugged, feeling powerful behind the wheel of the majestic buggy. "If she hasn't ever met this guy she hired? Then *I* could be him. *I* could be Charlie, the PI. It covers why I'm shadowing her husband. I handle her, get rid of her, and—"

"What do you mean," he said, giving me a sharp glance, " 'get rid of her'?"

"I hope I mean, I talk to her and she goes on her way."

He was staring at the memo. "What if she's already *met* Charlie?"

"Then maybe…well, there's other ways of getting rid of people."

The Broker sighed; his expression was one of extreme distaste. "Yes. Yes there are." He looked over at me, eyes half-lidded again. "I will have this Charlie character looked into. I'll have information available by late Monday afternoon. Call me before five at the same number. Don't do anything till then—don't return to your surveillance post, just stay in your hotel."

"The Holiday Inn."

His eyes and nostrils flared. "Hell, I hadn't thought of that. You're already in the hotel where the woman would be meeting you...."

"What's wrong with that? It's convenient."

He shook his head. "This world in Iowa City—it's too small, it's too cluttered."

"Tell me about it."

Broker's icy blue eyes bore down on me. "If I can confirm that our late friend Charlie was a single operative, and that he did not work out of the same city where Mrs. Byron lives, then there is a good chance that, *A*, she has never met him in person and dealt with him only over the phone, and, *B*, he will not immediately be missed, since he has no associates to miss him."

"You're assuming he worked alone—wasn't part of an agency."

"His business card implies a one-man operation. It's worth checking out."

I let some air out. "That *would* buy us a couple of days."

"Yes."

We rode along in silence for a while.

Then: "So what's in the manuscript, Broker?"

"What manuscript?"

"Don't play dumb. You don't play dumb at all well. The manuscript I'm expected to find and burn, after killing this philandering fucker."

"...It's a so-called non-fiction novel he's been working on."

"Well, that's his specialty, right? He's the *Collateral Damage* guy."

The Broker chuckled dryly. "Yes, in more ways than one, now. He's writing what he's described to others as his magnum opus—a non-fiction novel about a Mafia kingpin."

"Fuck," I said. "The girl's father?"

"Yes," the Broker said. "But ask me nothing more about it."

I didn't need to. But you had to hand it to the prof —not everybody can do research and get a blowjob at the same time.

SIX

The Holiday Inn's pool room was free of screaming kiddies on this Monday after Christmas. Families were homeward bound, and even my redheaded whirlpool partner was nowhere in sight—if she'd gone home, too, that would be a shame. I had worked up some pretty good fantasies about my thirty-something pick-up—I had a rough draft of a *Penthouse Forum* letter well under way in my mind.

But having the pool to myself—it was warm, maybe a little too warm—was a pleasure. My arms and legs cutting the water in this aquamarine echo chamber provided an otherworldly backdrop for the twenty laps I swam. The whirlpool felt good, really good, as my neck and upper back were fairly tense from all of last night's fun and games.

I didn't feel guilty about Charlie—he'd gone wading in and found himself in the deep end and that wasn't my doing—but I hadn't ever shot a guy right next to me before. Much of what I'd done in Vietnam had been as a sniper or in fire fights, and I'd seen plenty of bloody bodies nearby, but usually my fellow soldiers. As for that guy Williams I dropped the car on, well, obviously, the car was between him and me.

But I did have to face that a profession presented to

me by the Broker as clinical, surgical, and distant could have some haphazard, sloppy, and close-up ramifications. Didn't bother me, but this wasn't exactly what I expected. No biggie.

So I sat and relaxed for maybe half an hour in the swirling, soothing hot water, just enjoying the emptiness of the big room. I did a little time in the sauna, too, and was loose and comfortable and ready to start my day, come mid-morning.

The Broker had told me not to go back to the split-level till I'd talked to him, late afternoon; but I wasn't comfortable with the mess I'd left behind. So after I asked a few questions at the hotel's front desk, I headed out in the rental Maverick and picked up some cleaning stuff at the Kmart and headed over.

The stuff on the wall in the kitchen, on Charlie's side of the breakfast nook, was crusty and nasty, and took some muscle with the Brillo pad to make go away. I thought there'd be a bullet hole under there, but the slug must have still been in Charlie's noggin, possibly because where I'd shot him had been where the bone was pretty solid.

I cleaned up blackened blood from the linoleum, and some other encrusted grue, and the place soon looked like a kitchen and not a slaughterhouse. Probably nothing I'd done would have given a good forensics team any problem, but for a real estate agent or home buyer who came wandering in, nobody would be the wiser.

You might think I would do exactly what the Broker

told me to, and not stray in any way from his instructions; but the thing was, my ass was hanging out, not his. I was in the trenches and he was in his Caddy or at the Concort Inn or in some fancy mansion somewhere, so the decision was mine. If, this afternoon, the Broker wound up telling me to book it out of Dodge, and I'd have to leave that house behind, with blood spatter that wasn't about to be mistaken for a Jackson Pollock painting, then we'd just be asking for trouble.

Cleaning up that mess wasn't my only secret insubordination where the Broker was concerned: I had also failed to mention the half a dozen rolls of 35mm film of Charlie's that I'd found. My favorite game is poker, if I haven't mentioned it, and in poker you protect your hole card. And my hunch was those film rolls might be my ace.

In downtown Iowa City, I went to the photo shop the Holiday Inn desk clerk recommended, and left the rolls to be developed, with my photos ready tomorrow morning. I told the bored middle-aged guy behind the counter these were art shots, meaning naked women would be on some of them, and asked if that would be a problem. He said no, but it would be an extra twenty bucks.

By then it was close to noon and I followed another of the desk clerk's tips and walked over to a sandwich shop called Bushnell's Turtle, named for an early submarine and reflecting the style of sandwiches they served.

A record store, a book shop and Bushnell's were among half a dozen businesses in double-wide temporary buildings housed right out in the middle of Clinton Street at the end of East College, which was mostly blocked off for the construction of a pedestrian mall. I walked up a wheelchair-friendly ramp and into the unpretentious sandwich emporium, where you ordered at a counter from a chalkboard menu on the wall, got your food and found a table.

For winter break being on, the unpretentious sub shop was surprisingly busy, with straight customers from the business and retail community mixed in with hippie-ish college students. I'd already ordered when I spotted Annette Girard and Professor Byron, at a table over by the windows along Clinton, too late to make an inconspicuous retreat.

What the hell, I was just another college student, right? Longish hair, young face, no sweat. The question was, did I take a nearby table to eavesdrop on their conversation, or did I play it safe and position myself as far away from the pair as possible?

Do I have to tell you I took a table adjacent? I didn't figure there was much if any chance of Annette, who was deep in conversation with her loving prof, recognizing me from Sambo's, where we'd had our brief and not terribly memorable conversation.

They seemed to be past their meal or just having coffee, and I nibbled at a delicious sandwich (not a sub) where bratwurst and mozzarella and sauerkraut mingled nicely on rye. Beat the hell out of Slim Jims and Hostess cupcakes. And I could hear the couple pretty well.

"You have to open up, Annette," he was saying, the

oratorical baritone nicely modulated into whispery intimacy, "you have to be honest. That's part of the novel technique, you know."

Her head was tilted, her brunette hair pausing at the shoulders of her green and black paisley blouse on its way down her back. "Honesty in characterization and human behavior, sure…but otherwise, isn't all fiction a contrivance?"

An out-of-control eyebrow lifted in his hawkish face. "Of course it is, but when done well, a very high level of contrivance. Fiction is, after all, the lie that tells the truth. In a non-fiction work, you have to find multiple sources, and you often have to hew to accepted history, and that's a joke. But in fiction, you are inside the narrator's head, and in the first *person*, you share space with that narrator."

She was frowning. "But narrators in fiction can be unreliable. You've told me that."

"And that's permissible in a non-fiction novel, too, as long as the narrator, the main character, is *you*, and any exaggerations or lies are told in the context of your personal truth."

Wow. Was this guy full of shit!

"But I would encourage you *not* to lie," he was saying. "I would encourage you to engage your memories head-on. Confront them and conquer them. For example, you need to share with your reader every horrible thing your father ever did to you."

"K.J.," she said, "I don't *want* to relive all of that. It took me *years* of therapy to get past *any* of it."

"Then you *haven't* gone past it. Anyway, therapy is a

crutch; writing is catharsis. You put these experiences in your non-fiction novel, every single thing you witnessed, and when you're done, you can close the book on that entire sordid chapter. Literally."

I was confused. Who was writing the book on Annette's mob-boss father? Professor or student? Or were they collaborating?

"Anyway, we can discuss it this evening," Byron said, and rose, scooting his chair back and gathering his parka-style fur-lined khaki-green jacket; he was in a darker green sweater with the collars of a pale yellow shirt sticking out, and well-worn, just-another-radical blue jeans.

She asked him, "How many meetings do you have this afternoon?"

"Three. Should be safe to come around by six. We'll cook up some chili and put the Coltrane on and just talk this through."

She got up, too, getting into the familiar white coat with white fur collar, and that's when she recognized me. She brightened and met my eyes and I frowned at her as if I didn't know why the fuck she was looking at me—maybe not the most credible reaction from a straight guy having a beautiful girl gaze right at him.

"Hi!" she said.

"Hello," I said.

"You remember me—from Sambo's?"

The professor was studying me as if I were an exam paper written in crayon. Then he turned to Annette and asked, "What were *you* doing in Sambo's?"

"Having coffee, reading. When you had your meetings last night? You know it's just across from where I live."

"Ah. Sure." He put on a smile for me and nodded.

She held her hand out. "I didn't get your name. I'm Annette."

"Jack," I said, and shook hands with her.

The prof didn't offer his hand. But he did ask, with tight politeness, "What are you studying, Jack?"

"Just another English major," I said. "Nice to meet you, Annette…Professor Byron."

That seemed to please him, me knowing who he was. "So I don't need to introduce myself."

"No, I read your book about Vietnam. I'm a vet myself."

"How did you like it?"

"Vietnam really sucked."

"I meant my book."

"Oh! It was really good." I of course hadn't read it. But I figured that was all you needed to say to any writer to make a pal out of him.

And it worked.

"Well, thanks, Jack," he said, and now he finally held out his hand. "You interested in writing? You can always try out for the Workshop."

His grip was cold and clammy.

I said, "I hear it's tough, the competition."

"Oh yes, definitely." He nodded toward his favorite student. "But talent, like cream, does rise to the top."

Some writer, coining a phrase like that.

He was saying, "Annette here is going to be the next Flannery O'Connor."

"Hey, that's great." Who the fuck was Flannery O'Connor?

Must have been somebody pretty good, because Annette was blushing. That's what I said: blushing.

She nodded and headed out and he followed with no nod to me and I finished my sandwich. The Broker would love that, me talking literature with the target and the client's kid.

So that afternoon, with the world already growing dark outside my window, I called the Broker from the phone in my room at the Holiday Inn, and left out any report on my luncheon meeting at Bushnell's Turtle.

"You'll be relieved to know," the Broker said, *"that Charles Koenig has a small one-man private investigative agency in Des Moines, Iowa. He is divorced and has no children and is unlikely to be missed by anyone other than perhaps his landlord."*

"Cool," I said.

"And I would doubt that Mrs. Byron hired him in person. She lives in a small college town in Connecticut, where her husband first taught, before his writing career really took off. They, too, are a childless couple."

"You figure the wife looked for a PI in Iowa who could take on this case. Let her fingers do the walking, or anyway the long distance operator's fingers."

"Precisely. Hence, Charles Koenig of Des Moines."

I believe the Broker is the only person I ever heard speak the word "hence" in a sentence. Or not in a sentence, for that matter.

"So then I should stay," I said, "and finish what I came to do."

"I believe so…if you are willing to take a certain risk."

Well, let's see. Last night I had dragged a plastic-wrapped corpse down a hill so I could load it in a car trunk and drive to a truckstop and pass the stiff off to some other asshole. Yeah. I guessed I was up for a risk.

"What kind of risk, Broker?"

"You need to keep that meeting."

"What meeting?…Oh. You mean, the meeting Charlie was supposed to have with the professor's wife. And, what, I should pretend to be Charlie?"

"Yes. And why not? It's the lounge in your very own hotel. As you said yourself, how much more convenient could it be for you?"

"Well," I said, having second thoughts, "it won't be very convenient if your assumptions are wrong, and Mrs. Byron has in fact *met* Charlie. You could put me in a position of having to do something else unpleasant. More collateral damage."

"No. That shouldn't be a problem. Don't pass yourself off as Charlie, but as an operative in his employ."

Actually, that was a good idea. I'd already thought of it, but said nothing, not wanting to burst the Broker's bubble.

"Quarry, you know what Mr. Koenig was up to. Improvising your lines should be simple; a child could do it."

"Yeah, well, Christmas is over and all the kids have checked out of this dump, except for me, and I wasn't in any school plays or anything."

"You underestimate your abilities, my boy."

Broker was also the only person who had ever called

me "my boy." No, strike that: my drunken Uncle Pete called me that once, too, when I was six and he slipped his hands in my shorts. See how good I am at this nonfiction novel stuff?

"Okay, Broker," I said, "I'll do it. But what do I say to her?"

"Tell her you have the goods on her husband. That you'll gather all the materials and provide them soon."

"Listen, what's she doing here anyway? She's got an Iowa PI on the job who could report to her where she lives, which is Connecticut. What's going on?"

"She probably wants to be assured by Mr. Koenig — that's you — that her husband is indeed the philandering louse she assumes. And she plans to confront him about it, once having seen the evidence."

"Great. One more cast member in the stateroom."

"No. There won't be. You will tell her that you need several more days to collect the evidence. Send her home. Advise her in no uncertain terms that a confrontation with her husband is a mistake. That it will compromise her position in court."

"Would it?"

"Jesus Christ, young man!"

You guessed it: first time I ever heard that combination of words coming out of a fellow human; and it was a pretty rare outburst of any kind, coming from the Broker.

Who was saying, *"What difference does that make? You aren't really a private investigator working on a divorce case. You are merely trying to manipulate her ass into taking a goddamn hike. Understood?"*

"Sure," I said.

"Call me tonight and we'll discuss how the meeting with Mrs. Byron went, and we will decide, together, whether or not you should resume your activities."

"Okay."

We said goodbye and hung up.

So I had a shower and brushed my teeth and gargled and even splashed on a little Brut. I left off the long johns but my wardrobe was limited—I had a dark gray shirt and some jeans I hadn't worn yet, and that was the best I could do. I spent an hour in the coffee shop, having a bowl of chicken noodle soup for supper and reading the local papers. I don't follow sports or world affairs, but the funnies and the movie reviews took some time away.

By a quarter to seven, I was in the lounge, which was about the size of a high school classroom, only all red and black and with a bar in the middle and a little stage and dance floor in one corner. The band wasn't going on till nine, and a TV up high behind the bar showed Red Skelton doing Clem Kadiddlehopper and laughing at his own jokes. Within minutes, *Rowan & Martin's Laugh-In* replaced it, the comedy team exuding cheerful irony, and the collision of the two eras was pretty jarring. The sound wasn't on loud enough for me to make everything out from my booth, but I took in the sight gags and watched the girls in bikinis and body paint dance around and that passed the time.

A sultry alto said, "Hi."

I looked up and a pretty, and pretty familiar, face

was staring down at me: the redheaded bestower of hard ons from the whirlpool yesterday morning.

So she hadn't checked out; and she had, after all, said she was "sometimes in the bar" here at the Holiday Inn. And now my fantasies were poised to come true, *Penthouse Forum* here I come, only I was supposed to meet someone else, wasn't I?

Truth was, I wished I was meeting this blue-eyed redhead. She looked fucking great. Her tower of titian curls on top of that attractive roundish face, softened by the lounge lighting, her shapely body nicely served by a fuzzy yellow sweater, orange toreador pants and off-white heels. She had a yellow clutch purse in one hand and was gesturing to herself with the other, her nails the same orange as her tight slacks.

I smiled and did a kind of half rise from my seat in the booth. "Dorrie, isn't it? Gee, you look great."

Yes, I said "gee." But give me credit: I left off "whilli-kers."

Big white teeth formed a terrific smile. "You look good out of trunks....Actually, that sounded wrong, didn't it?"

I grinned. "Sounded just fine. Boy, do I wish I could ask you to join me, but I'm meeting somebody here."

"Actually, so am I. Trouble is, I didn't get a description."

My brain was making connections that yours probably already has. I said, "Dorrie...that isn't short for Dorothy, is it?"

Long lashes flashed over the blue eyes, which were almond shaped. "Well, yes...."

"You're Dorothy Byron?"

Now those blue eyes narrowed. "Yes. But you're not Charles Koenig, are you? You don't sound anything like him."

So she *had* dealt him over the phone.

I gestured for her to sit, and she slid in across from me. "I work for Mr. Koenig. He got called away on another case, out of state."

Way out of state.

She was smiling again. "Then *you're* handling this job?"

"That's right."

She shook her head, the red locks bouncing nicely, and said, "I feel so foolish. Here we were yesterday, sitting and talking and even...flirting, and...now I hardly know what to say."

"Say 'small world,' and let's take it from there."

The lounge was about half full now. Seemed to be young working people, in their later twenties and early thirties, on the prowl.

"This can be a real meat market," she said, casting her eyes around and frowning. "Could get fairly crowded. Is there somewhere else we could talk?"

"My room's a kind of mini-suite. There's a sitting area with a couch. We could send for some room service, if you haven't eaten."

"I'm not hungry, but I wouldn't mind the privacy. Maybe you could buy us a couple of beers, at the bar?"

I bought four cans of Pabst and then escorted Mrs. Byron out of the lounge and over to the elevators. She was a head-turner in that yellow sweater; she wore an old-fashioned brassiere, unusual in these bra-burning times, but I kind of dug its twin rocket style. Made me think of Mamie Van Doren and my first orgasm; probably was more memorable for me than Mamie, since Mamie wasn't there.

Now, I admit I did something stupid. I believe I was a little thrown by running into my whirlpool fantasy and having her turn out to be my target's missus. Right before I'd gone down to the lounge, I tossed my nine millimeter on the bed, and it was sitting there on the made bed against a pillow like the worst mint any maid ever left.

I'd spaced out about the damn thing, and still hadn't remembered the gun when I opened the door and she went on in ahead of me. But she saw it right away.

She turned and smiled, her eyes alive. "So private eyes *do* carry guns? Just like on TV!"

"We need protection," I said lamely. "But the management frowns on it when you carry one into a cocktail lounge."

I put the four beers on the coffee table by the couch, switched on the lamp (the overhead light was off, the bedroom nightstand lamp also on), and sat down. She deposited herself next to me, perhaps a little closer than most good-looking clients sit to their PI. Except on TV. She smelled very good. Perfume, but not too much. She was doing fine, *Penthouse Forum*-wise.

"So fill me in about the creep I'm married to," she said.

"There've been several girls go around to see him," I said, "but I think some are legitimately students. Couple guys have stopped by the cottage, too. He *is* an advisor, after all."

The upper lip of her full mouth curled upward. "He's been 'advising' for a very long time. I was one of his first. I was going to be a hell of a writer, myself, you know. The next Sylvia Plath."

I didn't know who that was, either, but I said, "I won't lie to you. I don't want to give you false hope—he is cheating."

She sat there with her fists clenched and her chin quivering and she stared at the wall across the way, which wasn't worth staring at really, having a nondescript winterscape framed there (screwed into the wall, to keep me from sticking it in my suitcase). Her eyes were hard but they were also wet, glistening with emotion, hate, love, the works.

I asked, "You didn't have any doubt, did you?"

She shook her head, red curls bouncing. "No. No. This is typical."

"Isn't this just about getting the goods on the guy? So you can finally pull the plug on this marriage and come out smelling like a rose on the financial end?"

She nodded.

I got up and went over to the cans of beer. I pulled the ring top on a Pabst and handed her the can and she sipped at it delicately. I pulled a ring top on another and returned to my place on the couch. I took a drink and set it on the floor. Wasn't that thirsty, but she was greedily consuming hers now, gone from sipping to gulping.

I said, "You don't have any kids, do you?"

"No. Didn't I tell you that? No."

She put the beer back on the end table, then got up and went over to the bed. She took the gun from the pillow and she turned around and the nine millimeter was huge in her orange-nailed hand. Her expression was a little crazy. But crazy enough.

She said, "You know I could just kill the son of a bitch."

"Not a good idea. Give me that."

"Or maybe *you* could. Would you kill him for me?" She seemed a little drunk. Maybe that hadn't been her first beer.

"No. That's not a toy."

She handed it to me, with a babyish pout that, oddly, was the first thing that had made her look her age. I took the weapon and held it in both hands; I'd never felt the metal so cold.

She plopped down next to me again. "One of us should kill that miserable prick."

"Yeah, well, not tonight."

Then she started crying, and I slipped an arm around her and she sobbed into my chest. Now and then she would say, "What's wrong with me? What's *wrong* with me?"

So I told her there was nothing wrong with her.

This went on a while.

Then she got up, suddenly, and ran to the bath-

room, taking her little purse along. I thought maybe
she was going to throw up, and I did hear the toilet
flush, but when she came back, she'd redone her make-
up, the mascara having run all to hell.

And she looked good again. Very good. Damn good.
And weirdly together, her face devoid of emotion,
devoid of anything but those attractive features, the
kind of blank prettiness you see in advertising.

She positioned herself in front of me.

"How old are you?" she asked.

I told her.

"I was in junior high when you were born," she said.

"I find that hard to believe."

"Would you believe grade school?"

The *Get Smart* reference made me laugh.

She took off her sweater, yanked it over her head
with magnificent casualness. She stared down at me;
so did the bullet bra.

"Would you believe," she said, overtly Maxwell Smart
now, "kindergarten?"

Her hands went behind her to undo the bra. I looked
away, the gun still in my hands. This was wrong. Fucking
the target's wife was wrong. I could get in ten kinds of
trouble. A hundred. She was a beautiful, sad, troubled
woman and she was taking her bra off and I was about
to get fucked several ways, not all of them good.

Her breasts had needed no help from the bullet bra.
Sure, they drooped just a little, but that was what my
hands were for. I reached up and caressed them, globes
that overflowed my fingers, her aureoles large and

puffy, and then I suckled them and the nipples grew hard and long, and I was hard and long, too, so I pulled her down on the couch and I climbed on her and we kissed or mostly I kissed her, nuzzling her neck and worshiping those breasts....

She slipped out from under me and had a naughty-child look as she stood there and wriggled out of the skin-tight slacks and revealed a healthy reddish pubic patch and when she half-turned to toss the slacks away, I saw how incredible and full her ass was, dimples so deep you could drink champagne out of them. If you had champagne.

Then she was on her knees and unbuttoning my pants and she gave the porno girls a real run for the money, sucking the tip, then sliding her mouth down, then up and down and licking around and making me wonder what the fuck that dipshit husband of hers was thinking. I almost came in her mouth, but she knew just when to stop and she smiled up at me, those eyes incredibly blue, and got to her feet and walked to the bed, hip-swaying till I was drunk with it, and it was only about six steps.

She grabbed a pillow out from under the covers and put it under her hips and lifted herself to me and opened herself like a pink flower in a red bush, eyes glistening, pussy too, and she asked, "I'm not so bad, am I? Not so bad."

"No," I said. "Just enough."

The rest you probably read in *Penthouse Forum*.

SEVEN

We finished the four beers, though Dorrie had three of them, and had another enthusiastic fuck, this time on the couch with the curvy gal sitting on my lap facing me, and she was pretty drunk at that point and her face wasn't looking so hot, no make-up and kind of saggy, but her body held up fine and anyway I hadn't been laid in a couple months.

She gathered her clothes and padded into the bathroom to freshen up. I heard the shower going and thought about joining her, but my dick was as red as a radish and I thought the better part of valor was just to get my own clothes on and call myself lucky.

Her purse had been in there, so when she emerged she was fairly put together, and I suggested we go downstairs for a nightcap. I had an ulterior motive, which was to make sure she didn't spend the night in my room—I needed more freedom than that—and I was pleased when she accepted my invitation.

She had a Vodka Collins and I had a gimlet while we sat in a booth and played PI and client. The "band"— a guy with a guitar and a gal with a keyboard doing horrific soft rock with drum-machine backing—was at least not very loud. The guitarist was perched on a stool and wore a velour jumpsuit and pink shirt; he smiled and sang back-up. The girl, in a gypsy-pattern peasant dress and seated behind her keyboard, did the lead vocals in a whispery folky voice just perfect for "Which Way You Goin', Billy?" Perfect in the sense that "Which Way You Goin', Billy?" would make great background music for driving off a bridge.

The tiny dance floor, however, was packed with couples in upright copulation mode, and they soaked up some of the sound, at least.

Dorrie was sucking on the orange slice from her Tom Collins glass. If I hadn't just been fucked royal, twice, that might have been provocative.

I sipped my gimlet. "I'll send you the photos."

She shook the reddish tower of curls. "No. I want to *see* them. I want you to talk me through them."

"Huh?"

"Tell what else you saw, you know, in relation to the photos."

I frowned. "I really think it would be better if you went back to Connecticut and let me send you the photos and report to you over the—"

"I want to see those photos." She stretched out a palm, like a child demanding candy. "I want to see them…*right here*."

I thought about it. "Okay, that's not a problem. They'll be developed by noon tomorrow. We can meet in the coffee shop for lunch, and then you can check out and go home."

The blue eyes, though a little bleary, tightened and grew hard. "No. I want to see that bastard. I want to rub the evidence in his goddamn face."

"Not such a good idea. Listen, I'm experienced at

this, or anyway Mr. Koenig is. I can tell you, with absolute certainty, that having contact with your husband, harassing him and so on, will only hurt your cause in court."

Her chin crinkled—she wasn't was about to cry or anything, this was more like a pout, and not as fetching as ones she'd given me earlier, back when she was stripping for me.

"If you want simple revenge," I said, "you could throw the photos in his face, kick him in the nuts, do whatever you like. But if you hired our agency because you want to build a divorce case against this cheater, then let me do the job I'm being paid for. And as delightful as spending time with you is, you need to get out of my way."

She frowned. "You're not finished with the job?"

I shook my head. "I may not be. I haven't seen the developed photos yet. I took some through the window catching your husband in *flagrante delicto*."

"That's French for fucking some whore, right?"

"More or less. But I'm frankly not as good with a camera as Mr. Koenig, and it was at night, and I didn't have a flash, going through hazy curtains—we need to see what I got. I may have to go back for more."

"And I'm…I'm in your way."

The couple on stage was doing a version of "Raindrops Keep Fallin' On My Head." Try to imagine how wretched it was. Nice try, but no.

"Iowa City is a small town," I said. "If your husband even sees you around here, you may blow it for me. Please let me do my job."

That was a genuine plea: *please let me do my job*.

"Okay," she said, and shrugged helplessly. "Listen, I, uh…I'm going up to my own room to spend the night. That doesn't offend you or anything?"

"No."

"It's just…I've kind of gotten used to sleeping alone."

"Fine."

"You're not hurt?"

I gave her my best smile. "No. I had a wonderful time. This is a night I'll never forget."

Her smile was rumpled, but she really was very pretty. Not that blank, advertisement pretty I'd seen earlier, but a woman with lovely features and an intelligence that the beers and the vodka hadn't completely diminished.

She asked, "Really? Even though I have a few miles on me?"

"I'd be glad to help you rack up a few more, any time."

That made her laugh a little, and she slid out of the booth and so did I. The duo was slaughtering "Fire and Rain." Really should be a law.

I walked her to the elevators and up to her room. She gave me a nice kiss, soft and sweet, and unlocked her door and hip-swayed in, at least a little drunk.

Back in my room, I collected the nine millimeter and stuffed it in my waistband. This goddamn job was getting out of hand. From what I'd overheard, Annette would have gone over to the prof's around six this evening. If she did not stay the night, I might be able to get this turkey shot.

So within an hour, I was back at my window in the split-level, with the only change the addition of the little portable TV, its rabbit-ears adjusted to bring in Johnny Carson as best as possible. I kept the volume pretty low. The show had just started and Johnny and Ed and Doc were just fooling around, no guests yet.

Surprisingly, I was fairly alert. I'd slept most of the afternoon, starting when I got back from lunch at Bushnell's Turtle up till my phone call to Broker, so I was ready to put in a night shift. Annette's white Corvette was at the curb, meaning she was still in there, getting tutored in one way or another.

Maybe fifteen minutes later, while Johnny Carson was interviewing Charles Nelson Reilly, I thought for a second I'd fallen asleep and was dreaming, and not in a good way. A car had just pulled up behind the Corvette, a Plymouth Barracuda with a rental sticker in the back window. I hadn't seen this vehicle, among the several thousand that seemed to have shown up at the cobblestone cottage, but I sure knew the driver who got out and strode up the sidewalk: Dorrie Byron herself, the lovely woman who had so recently fucked my dick raw.

Hadn't she had *enough* fun for one night?

She was dressed as before, the orange of her toreador pants flashing under a white fur coat, possibly a mink, meaning she'd already got at least some money out of the prof. My mouth had dropped and it was all I could do not to yell out the window at her, *What the hell do you think you're doing, lady?*

Johnny was laughing at Charles, and I turned the

little portable down so I could make out what was coming. Already I could hear her fist pounding on the front door. She paused and then pounded some more.

Finally the door opened and yellow light poured out around the tall figure of her husband, in his maroon terrycloth bathrobe.

As before, voices carried in the crisp, cold air as if from a stage to a theater's audience.

"Darling!" he said. "What a wonderful surprise!"

"It was terrible spending Christmas without you," his wife said. "I can stay till New Year's if you like!"

"That would be wonderful!"

He sort of seemed to be shouting, and of course I knew why. Anyway, the prof was now enfolding his wife in his arms and they were kissing, fairly passionately considering he was a philandering prick and she was the wronged wife seeking a divorce, not to mention solace by having sex with innocent young boys like myself.

With an arm around her, and considerable concern, he ushered her into the house and shut the door. He'd hardly done that when Annette, naked flesh and a dark pubic thatch flashing under her unbuttoned white leather coat, a pile of clothing in her arms, went running in her bare feet on the snowy ground along the side of the house just at the edge of the gravel driveway. She scrambled around to the driver's side of the Corvette and fumbled unlocking the door, but then was in and behind the wheel and taking off quickly though not peeling out or anything, no burned rubber to attract the attention of the professor's new house guest.

Now I might have found this amusing if I hadn't noticed something beside clothing in her arms as she scurried out from around back in French farce fashion. She also had a box, the kind of box a ream of typing paper comes in, and this she held as preciously as the items that would cover the pale flesh under the white leather.

Was that the book? *The* book?

My job here wasn't just eliminating the professor, after all, but getting rid of the non-fiction novel that would embarrass and expose Annette's father back in Chicago.

I quickly exited the split-level and ran down to the garage next door and got in the Maverick and took off after Annette. I admit to having no plan. The last thing I wanted to do, or for that matter that our client would want me to do, was harm this girl. But the possibility of me dealing with Professor Byron tonight, with his loving wife around, was nil; and maybe I could find some way to pry that manuscript away from Annette without blowing my cover or having to kill her lovely ass.

Confused as hell, feeling like I was in way over my head, I made sure at least one car was between me and the brunette's Corvette as I tailed her. Hell, it was no secret where she was going. And, sure enough, before long she was pulling into her slot at the little apartment building in Coralville. She had taken time to button the white leather coat, so no major flashes of skin or bush were on display as she got out of the vehicle and trotted up the stairs to the second level and sealed herself in her apartment.

I pulled into the Sambo's lot again.

Christ, I had no idea what to do. Would I really be reduced into breaking into that girl's apartment, subduing her somehow, and stealing that manuscript? What, wearing a ski mask like the Broker suggested? What was I, a second-story man now? A burglar? Didn't I have *some* goddamn dignity?

I sat for maybe fifteen minutes trying to think, but when my stomach began to growl—all I'd had for supper was a bowl of soup—I thought, *Fuck it*, and went on in to the Sambo's.

This was still winter break, and fairly late at night, so the garish, brightly illuminated orange-and-white restaurant was underpopulated, enough miserable kids in orange caps and orange-and-white uniforms for every customer to have a personal waiter or waitress.

I damn near laughed, though, when I saw two big black guys, who looked like they'd wandered off the set of *Cotton Comes to Harlem*, sitting at the endless counter. One wore a green hat with a gold band, tilted rakishly, and a green long-sleeve shirt and green-and-brown plaid bell bottoms. The other wore a similar hat, but black with a leather band and a red feather, and a red shirt with pointy collars and deep-brown corduroy bells. Both had major Afros and Groucho-wide mustaches, and each had folded a leather (one black, one brown) topcoat carefully over the free stool next to him. They were drinking coffee and having pancakes and every side you can imagine. Tiger butter and all.

Call me a racist if you like, but this urban pair sitting in a Sambo's made a wonderful sight gag.

Anyway, I found a booth and ordered my own big breakfast, and I sat by myself, thinking about how fucked-up this job had become and seriously considering risking the wrath of the Broker and bailing. Every time I turned around, some new wrinkle, some new conflict, presented itself. Whatever happened to *Wait till he's alone, go in and pop him and leave?*

Of course this had never been that kind of job. It had always had that little extra "challenge" (as the Broker put it) of destroying a certain manuscript, and wondering what to do next had my head swimming.

I was well into my late-night breakfast when Annette came into Sambo's, a green pants suit and ruffly blouse taking the place of naked skin under her white leather coat. She saw me at once, and smiled, and came over.

"Nice to see a friendly face, Jack," she said, and slid in across from me. "Mind if I join you?"

Kind of hard to say no when she already had, so I said, "Sure," and asked, "Rough day?"

"Don't ask! Horrible. Simply horrible."

I touched a napkin to my lips, then asked, "Want to order something?"

"Oh yes, I'm *starved.*"

A waitress came over, and the "starved" girl ordered a dinner salad with oil and vinegar, and a cup of coffee.

I was almost done with my food, so I shoved it to one side and asked, "Trouble with your book?"

"Kind of." She shook her head and dark brown hair danced on her shoulders. "It's tough, collaborating."

"Is that what you're doing? Collaborating?"

"...Not exactly."

"Your book, your non-fiction novel—is Professor Byron co-writing it?"

Again she shook her head. "Not really. I think of it as a collaboration because he's given me so much advice, so much support. We've become very close."

"Really. Doesn't he have a kind of reputation for…if I'm out of line, just say so, but…"

Her salad came.

She said, "I'm not in love with Professor Byron or anything. We're just good friends."

I could use a good friend who looked like her who would blow me.

"But I won't deny," she said, "that he's something of a satyr."

"A what?"

She smiled, more to herself than at me. "He is known to hit on his female students."

"A letch, you mean. Dirty old man."

She smiled, maybe a tad embarrassed; she forked some salad. "He's a wonderful, talented writer, and I'm glad to have a relationship with him. He's mature but young at heart. Anyway, I'm not looking for a…a husband, or any kind of serious relationship. He's a virile, charismatic man, and I'm single right now, and we are very close, very, very close friends, so…what's the harm?"

"Nothing, I'd say. You have your eyes open, anyway."

"Yeah, but…" She shook her head yet again, and those big brown eyes really were open—wide. "…tonight, out of *nowhere*, his wife showed up. God, she's a crazy person. A shrew. Just a horrible monster."

"How long have you known her?"

"Oh, we've never met. But K.J. has told me about her."

"Oh." I sipped iced tea. "Listen, I'm interested in this non-fiction novel concept. I've fooled with writing since I was in grade school. I mean, I know I'm not in your league, but I am interested in pursuing it."

She shrugged. "Glad to help, if I can." Another bite of salad. Her lips were very full and quite beautiful; female lips that stay beautiful while chewing food are to be treasured. "What can I tell you?"

"You're writing your own story—of your own life."

Eager nod. "Yes."

"And the professor isn't doing any of the writing. He's just guiding you."

"That's right."

"Well…how old are you?"

"Twenty-two."

"Okay. Isn't twenty-two a little young to *have* a life story to write? I mean, don't people do their memoirs right before they croak, generally?"

She laughed and it was musical, contrasting with faint Muzak piped in. "I had an unusual childhood. An unusual life all the way around."

"Really?"

She nodded. "My father is someone…famous. Or infamous."

"Oh. So it's a celebrity story. What it's like to be the kid of a celebrity. Cool."

She frowned, shook her head. "Not so cool. My father…you've heard of Lou Girardelli?"

"You mean…Sinatra's pal?"

That caught her off-guard and she laughed again. "Yes. Yes, Sinatra's pal."

"You mean you've met Sinatra?"

"Oh yes. He's charming, most of the time. The nicest manic depressive I know."

I thought, *I bet* he's *mature but young at heart, too….*

I asked, "Isn't that a dangerous story to write?"

She leaned forward, her eyes earnest. "You mean, wouldn't my father be displeased? Yes, he will. But I'm his daughter. He'll dismiss my story, in public, as a drug-addled fantasy from an estranged daughter, trying to make a fast buck by writing a 'tell-all.' You see, I don't know any of the criminal details of his life. I only know the home life. But that's enough. Really enough."

"You said 'drug-addled.'…You don't seem very drug-addled to me."

Her eyebrows lifted and she looked down at her mostly eaten salad. "I was into pot and pills in high school. It did get bad, I won't deny it, and I had to be hospitalized for a while. But I'm fine now."

"You seem awfully well-adjusted, for all you've been through."

She brightened. "Thanks. And K.J., Professor Byron, he's helping me throw off the…the final *shackles* of my past."

I nodded. "Write about it, and get it out of your system, you mean?"

"Exactly. Exorcize the demons. Everyone has them. I just happened to have one as a father."

I had a drink of tea, then I asked, "So now that Mrs. Professor has shown up, what's your plan?"

She sighed. "I guess I'll burrow into my little apartment and work by myself till I hear from K.J. In any event, I won't work any more tonight. I can use some sleep."

She reached for her check but I touched her hand.

"Let me get it," I said. "You're a cheap enough date."

With a laugh, she said, "Thanks," and slid out of the booth.

"See you, Jack. You're easy to talk to."

"You are, too."

Then she was gone.

The iced tea had run through me, so I went back to the men's room, thinking that since I knew Annette would not be returning to the professor's until she was summoned, I could wait till tomorrow before my next step. After Dorrie Byron left the prof's pad to take her meeting with me, and pick up those photos, I wouldn't show up, being busy back at the cobblestone cottage, killing her straying husband and destroying his manuscript.

Because my theory now was that this wasn't about the manuscript Annette had carried out of the prof's at all. No. The prof was writing his *own* in-depth book about Lou Girardelli, and Annette was just one phase of his research. He was encouraging her, building her up, to get more out of her, and not just blowjobs. I was convinced the prof had a book in progress that Annette knew nothing about.

And *that* was the manuscript I'd been sent to destroy.

I paid the check and was coming around the building when I spotted those two black guys again, the super-cool dudes in the threads and pimp hats. They were at the rear of what I assumed was their car, a Cadillac Fleetwood Eldorado like the Broker's, except bright red with white sidewalls, and they were stuffing something into the trunk.

Annette Girard.

EIGHT

The good news was the girl wasn't dead. The bad news was everything else.

Well, maybe some more good news at that: they hadn't seen me. Coming around the side of the restaurant like I had, I'd been able to slip behind some snowy bushes, and plaster myself against the stucco wall and peek around.

The two black guys, whose presence at Sambo's seemed ever less comical, were in their dark leather coats and had just completed dropping Annette into the trunk like a big golf bag that took both their best efforts. Since the girl probably weighed 130 pounds, those efforts had been expended in part by subduing her, though not knocking her out or chloroforming her (even these guys didn't know where to get chloroform), just slapping some duct tape over her mouth, a slash of it covering much of her lower face, her eyes wide and wild above, and very much conscious. Her wrists were also duct-taped and so were her ankles. She wasn't struggling now, fairly paralyzed with fear, I'd say.

Then the one in the red hat, who was a little bigger than his partner, held up a palm toward the one in the green hat, who gave him, I shit you not, a high five. The slap rang in the chill night like a gunshot, and they both chuckled, the bigger one's voice higher, the slightly smaller one having more of a low growly laugh.

They seemed pretty proud of overcoming a coed in a Sambo's parking lot. Some fucking people.

I watched like an Indian behind a tree, scouting a cowboy campfire, as the red Fleetwood roared to life, the red-hat kidnapper behind the wheel (apparently color-coordinating). The driver made more noise revving up his engine than I would have, had I just thrown a live girl in my trunk (or a dead one for that matter), but no one noticed except me. Then they backed out of their space and drove out of the lot, turning left toward the Coralville strip.

I knew where they were heading, or was at least pretty sure, and by "knew" I mean what city, which since the city was Chicago maybe was a little vague at that.

Anyway, I got into the Maverick and went after them. I was fond of Annette, but that wasn't why I took what I guess you'd call pursuit. Even on my first job, I knew this was not standard operating procedure; but I had inadvertently learned that her father was our client, and this was after all our client's daughter being driven away to face a variety of possibilities, the most benign of which wasn't very benign.

I'd been told by the late Des Moines PI Charles Koenig that Chicago mobster Lou Girardelli was in the middle of a drug turf war with black gangsters. You didn't have to be Sherlock Holmes or even Charles Koenig to figure out these two black thugs had been sent to kidnap the mob boss's daughter for fun and profit. Might be a straight ransom kidnapping, might be a trade-off for turf rights (you get the girl, we get the South Side), might be they wanted to fuck her, torture her, fuck her again, kill her slow, maybe fuck her one more time, and dump her on daddy's porch. That last one wasn't the benign possibility, by the way.

Two blocks down and a few more over were the east and west ramps onto Interstate 80. The Caddy would almost undoubtedly take the I-80 E ramp, and head toward Illinois and sweet home Chicago. I hadn't thought much farther ahead than that, except for the possible futures for Annette outlined above, and had nothing specific in mind.

I did know that if that pair of soul brothers made it to Chicago with Annette, I would not be able to lend the girl a hand. I needed them to interrupt their trip with a stop. It was a good four hours and change to Chicago, and considering they'd just been in a Sambo's, both guys would need to piss and/or shit, sooner or later. Probably sooner.

I was nervous. I don't apologize for that. I'd been through rough stuff in the jungle, but a kind of adrenaline high plus the camaraderie of your fellow soldiers got you into it and then through it, and sniper duty was a whole other deal, more a Zen kind of state where nerves didn't come into play, not if you wanted to survive.

I liked surviving. It was about all I valued. I'd seen plenty of evidence supporting the notion that life and death were meaningless, and God was either non-existent or uninterested, but what was wrong with

breathing? Didn't a decent meal and getting laid and
watching something funny or exciting on television or
reading a good western and did I mention getting laid,
didn't that all beat nothingness inside a box six feet
under all to shit? So I tend to come down strong on the
survival side.

And these two guys were big. They were also black,
and fuck you, I'm no racist, I fought alongside black
guys and I bet you didn't; so *you* go up against a couple
of streetwise soldiers for the Black Mafia, taller than
you, fifty pounds each on you, probably packing all
kinds of shiny steel. Either one of those guys could
fuck me up in a fair fight, and together they could
throw me down and kick me till a busted rib punc-
tured something and I drowned in my own goddamn
blood.

So, hell yes, I was nervous.

But not scared, really. My nine millimeter was on
the seat next to me, the radio tuned to an FM station
where the Beaker Street program was going, DJ Clyde
Clifford doing zonked-out intros to album cuts against
electronic space music right out of *Forbidden Planet*,
and while I hadn't done weed since Nam, Clyde and
his offbeat music choices chilled me out nicely, though
"In-a-Gadda-Da-Vida" (coming up on the drum solo)
probably meant we again had a disc jockey who needed
a bathroom break.

The landscape was an ivory-washed blue once more,
the snow frozen in odd clumps and clusters on the
terraced earth along I-80, the temperature having
gone up and down today, thawing, freezing, thawing,

freezing, making modern art out of precipitation. The trucks were blowing past me again, and the traffic in general was heavier. This didn't bother me, and even encouraged me, because it meant I could stay several car lengths away from the Fleetwood and not be spotted. An interstate in general was proving a great place to tail somebody; so what if you and somebody else were going in the same direction?

Several exits for gas and restaurants slipped by, including the green dinosaur and the Cove. We drove such a distance that even "Vida" ended, and the Vanilla Fudge doing "Season of the Witch" took over, filled with screams and whimpering, and though normally I dug that cut, I ditched Clyde for an easy listening station. Frank, Dino and Sammy were more like it, anyway. I was doing a job for Frank's pal, Lou, right? Even if Lou didn't know it.

As Frank sang "My Kind of Town," we blew past the Quad Cities where the Broker and his Concort Hotel were. Then, with Bobby Darin doing "Once in a Lifetime," just west of the Mississippi River and north of Walcott, Iowa, they pulled off at a dinky oasis economically called the I-80 Truck Stop—two diesel pumps, four gas pumps, a small white enamel gas station attached to a slightly bigger restaurant.

Shit.

I'd been hoping for one of the state-run rest stops. With a little luck, at one of those—which were just toilets and vending machines—I might have what I needed to deal with Annette's captors, which was no audience.

I pulled off anyway. Were they going to eat again? Wasn't that Sambo's feast enough for them? Maybe they worked up an appetite overpowering a twenty-two year-old college girl.

The Fleetwood pulled into one of the slots along the row of restaurant windows. If these guys had a brain between them, they would take the nearest window onto that stall. I stopped at the gas pumps, cut the engine, got out and instructed the kid to fill me up with regular, which was pushing forty cents a gallon, highway fucking robbery. Then I went into the gas station portion of the interconnected buildings. They sold some trucker gear, and I bought a rabbit-lined brown nylon zipper jacket.

I'd left my corduroy jacket in the car. While I had no reason to think those two had noticed me at Sambo's, I also had no reason not to. The gas station had all kinds of toiletries, so I was able to buy a tube of Brylcreem and a comb. I went into the Truckers Only restroom, which had showers and an array of sinks, at one of which I dumped water into my hands and dumped it on my head. Then I used the Brylcreem, and a little dab didn't do me, no, I squeezed that shit out of the tube and combed my hair into a style that must have been at least as effective a birth control method as the Pill.

After paying for the gas, and getting an odd look from the young attendant, since I seemed to be a different customer now, I drove the Maverick over into another of the stalls. I was still flying by the seat of my pants, and when I got out and then walked past the parked red Fleetwood, knowing that the girl was in that trunk, I wondered if I could somehow get her out of there and toss her in the Maverick and just book it the hell away.

Problem was, her black escorts were seated at the window adjacent, as I'd figured they would (apparently they did have at least one brain between them). What was I supposed to do, shoot the lock off the trunk? I'd never tried that, and I doubt you have. I would have probably killed the girl and then those assholes would have come tumbling out the restaurant and jumped my ass, if they didn't just fire through the window at me.

Or I could shoot out the window of the Fleetwood, reach in and open the car and hope this vehicle had a trunk release button; that should be standard on a Caddy, right? But where? Under the dash, or in the glove compartment, and oh by the way, those black bastards have killed me by now.

So I did what any other hero hoping to rescue a fair maiden would do: I went in and had a piece of coconut cream pie. I could use the sugar rush. The waitress was young and cute but not at all interested in a guy with greasy kid's stuff on his hair. I ate my pie and drank my iced tea and did my best to listen to the two black guys in the booth right behind me.

Green hat: "Man, why not have some fun? Enos is gonna kill her ass, ain't he?"

Red hat: "He might. He might not. Do you sit at the table with Enos and the others, planning shit? No. Do I? No fuckin' way. We muscle. We goddamn good at it, but we muscle."

"We could go someplace with her. Some motel or some shit. We tell her we let her go, she's nice to us. We can fuck her one at a time or each take a hole."

They were whispering, by the way. But I was right behind them, and even if I'm filling in a word here or there, trust me—I'm giving you more than the gist.

Red Hat: "You think she go for that?"

Green Hat: "Why not? These white girls, these college girl cunts, they sluts, they whores. And they curious about whether black men is all hung like fuckin' horses, which I am and if you ain't, that's your problem."

The previous had been mixed with laughter and was clearly kidding, but the guy in the red hat said, "Fuck you and the horse cock you rode in on."

"Aw, come on, don't be a dick. You think she won't bargain?"

"Then what?"

"Then what, we tape her up again and take her to the boss."

"And she tells the boss his boys diddled her up and down? How's Enos gonna like that shit? What if Enos wants to *trade* the little twat? He might want her not fucked up and shit."

"Well…I just sayin'."

"You say too much, Leon."

"Kiss my ass, Charlie."

Not another Charlie!

They didn't talk much after that. They had big platters of chicken and fries show up soon after. Yes, they ate chicken—fucking sue me. They ate chicken like all the white truckers around them were eating chicken. Jesus.

And speaking of truckers, the I-80 restaurant was packed. The I-80 Truck Stop was popular and the possibility of me getting these two alone was somewhere between slim and none.

So I finished my coconut cream pie and iced tea, and paid the check, and went back to my Maverick and started it up and sat waiting. Within minutes, Leon in his green hat and Charlie in his red hat returned to the Eldorado. Charlie again drove; maybe it was his wheels.

I let them leave the lot and take their ramp before I picked up the chase, if you can call it that. I was praying that that chicken, which everybody in the truck stop was gobbling down like junkies jamming heroin, was as greasy as it had looked and smelled going by on waitress trays. That might mean a bathroom break would come our way, and with just a little luck, that would also mean a state-run rest stop, not a restaurant or gas station.

Since I hadn't seen either of them go off to the can, that meant those guys had the Sambo's breakfast in their guts mingling with that greasy chicken, and if that combination didn't explode into flying shit sooner or later, I didn't know my chemistry.

And less than forty-five minutes later, the Eldorado pulled into a little rest stop right off the Interstate.

So did I.

The brick building was small, a glorified shed. Through its smoky glass front doors glowed vending machines. A car and two open spaces were between the Eldorado and where I sat in the Maverick. I watched the now hatless Leon rush in, holding his belly. Casually I got out of the Ford and walked into the little rest stop building. I had been able to glimpse a disgusted Charlie sitting at the wheel of the parked Eldorado, beating the heel of his hand against the steering wheel, possibly in tune to something on his radio. The engine was going.

Inside, the vending machines and a bulletin board that was mostly a big map of Illinois were in between the doors marked MEN at left and WOMEN at right. Next to the WOMEN's door, just past the bulletin board, was another door that said PRIVATE.

I tried that door; it was locked. Over in one corner was an abandoned mop and pail, and a yellow plastic sign, an inverted V that said, CLOSED FOR CLEANING. This sign was up against the brick wall at my far right, just shoved there when a lazy employee took off work. This theory was validated by a notice on the bulletin board above the map:

NO ATTENDANT IN ATTENDANCE
10 PM — 6 AM.

That seemed awkward to me: "ATTENDANT"/"ATTENDANCE." Maybe I was hanging around the Writers' Workshop too much. Anyway, it was nice news, knowing I didn't have to deal with some poor janitor.

A guy came out of the MEN's, a pasty-faced middle-aged character in a rumpled blue suit and no tie, probably a salesman. I had my hand on the restroom door, half-open, taking my time going in, watching the blue suit go out and cross to that other car parked between mine and the Eldorado.

Good.

I went in.

Man, it smelled like shit in there. Okay, that's no surprise, but the chicken clearly wasn't sitting well with Leon, who was in one of two stalls making a lot of noise, some of it from his mouth. I waited for him. *Pee-yew*, I thought.

I took a position at the electric hand drier, which I turned on, initiating its electronic wheeze, just as he finally flushed. My back was to him, so he couldn't see I was wearing black Isotoner gloves and that the nine millimeter was in my right hand. I was hoping he had some sense of hygiene, because this would be easier if he did.

And, bless him, Leon went to a sink and began to wash up. "Man!" he said, and smiled over at me, flashing two gold teeth under the thickness of mustache. "I ain't gettin' any younger."

I turned and showed him the nine millimeter and said, "You might not be, at that."

He frowned; I've never seen more wrinkles in a face that young. He couldn't have been more than twenty-five.

"Are you shitting me, white boy?"

"No. You've done enough shitting for both of us. This is a straight robbery. Behave yourself and we'll be fine."

"You got your fuckin' *nerve*—"

I was in the corner between the sinks and the drier, good positioning in case Charlie got impatient or curious or something and came in looking for Leon.

"Very slowly," I said, "take off that coat. I can see there's something heavy in the right pocket, and since it's probably a gun, I'd encourage you to go nowhere near it."

"Fuck you!"

But he did it. He unbuttoned the jacket and folded it in half and laid it carefully across the sink, not wanting it to go onto the bathroom floor. Couldn't blame him.

"Now carefully empty your pockets onto that jacket."

He did. He had various stuff, including a fat diamond money clip, but what attracted my attention was the straight razor.

"Okay. Now get into that stall. Make it the one you used."

That was the closer of the two.

I didn't have to ask him to put his hands up. As my gun and I moved forward, he backed up toward the stall, and edged in, his eyes moving fast. He was thinking. He was planning.

"You wait five minutes," I said, "before you come out. I'm going to leave you your watch. You exit any sooner, and you're a dead man."

Something in his eyes relaxed.

"No problem," he said. "Just take my money and split. Everybody got to make a living."

"I like your new attitude. Stay with that."

He was in the stall now.

"Turn around," I told him.

"Don't do that, man. Don't knock me out! You don't need to do that shit."

"I won't. Turn around."

With a sigh of defeat and a disgusted sneer, he did.

"You can put your hands down," I said.

He did, and that relaxed him.

When I cut his throat with the razor, the arterial spray got on the wall and maybe a little on him, but not a drop on me. I hate razors and knives, but they do have their uses, if you take a little care.

I arranged him on the floor so that he knelt over the bowl, where he did the rest of his bleeding into the water. That gave him the look of a guy throwing up, though the scarlet Rorschach test dripping on the wall was a dead giveaway.

I shut him in there.

The razor I threw in the sink. I wouldn't be needing it. His leather coat I stuffed in the trash receptacle. Finally I glanced at myself in the mirror, checking for blood spatter I may have missed: nothing. My horrific greased-back hair was still in place.

In the outer area of the rest stop, through those smoky glass doors, I could see that no other cars had pulled in. I went over and grabbed that yellow plastic V saying CLOSED FOR CLEANING and placed it out in front of the MEN's, but not blocking the path.

Quickly I went out to the Eldorado and knocked on the driver's side window.

Charlie's mustached face glowered at me; he didn't

have his red hat on now, and his head was shaved. Behind his window, he said, "What the fuck?"

I made a "roll the window down" motion, and he powered down the glass and said, "Do I know you?"

Hope not.

"Listen, your friend is in the restroom and he's very sick. He asked me to come and get you."

"Aw, shit, what is it now?"

That was to himself, or to the absent Leon; but I answered, anyway. "I don't know, but he's puking his head off. He said he was throwing up blood!"

Now some alarm came into Charlie's face, and I stood back as he shut off the Caddy engine and shoved the keys in his pocket and threw open the door and rushed into the rest stop and on into the bathroom, past the yellow inverted-V CLOSED floor sign, with me on his heels.

He opened the stall door and said, "Charlie, what the fuck?"

I shoved the nine millimeter against the small of his back, right up against the leather of his coat, which muffled the blast, not as good as a silencer, but not bad under the circumstances. His spine must have been severed, because he dropped like a bag of laundry on top of the kneeling Leon. Just to make sure, I put one through his head, and red and white and gray and green splatter daubed the porcelain and steel fixtures, glistening and shimmering like spilled liquid mercury.

Somebody else could pull into the rest stop any time, and I had no desire to rack up collateral damage.

So I worked fast, searching Charlie's coat pockets, coming up with a big shiny .357 magnum and the Caddy keys. In hopes of robbery being the initial motive the local cops came up with (eventually the mob connection would surface), I performed the distasteful task of checking Charlie's pants pockets, too. And, listen, it had already smelled bad in there, thanks to Leon's chicken attack. With Charlie vacating in his trousers after I blew his spine apart, this was turning into a real hellhole.

But Charlie had his own fat money clip, and between Charlie's and Leon's cash, I gave it a quick count of three thousand and change. Not a bad perk, and the diamonds on Leon's clip were real. I left the razor behind, still down in the sink. Not my style.

I did stay long enough to clean up one mess: I ran some water and got that Brylcreem out of my hair, then stuck my head under the electric hand drier for a few seconds. When I got that girl out of the trunk, I didn't want to look like a total fucking nerd.

NINE

When I opened the Caddy trunk, its light clicked on and the girl gazed up at me with those big brown eyes, and a wide range of human emotion—fear, surprise, relief, hope, confusion—flashed one at a time through them, each punctuated by a blink. Under the duct tape gag, she made an *unnnngggh* that, while not as impressive as what her eyes had done, was fairly communicative at that.

"No questions," I said, as I peeled off the tape. "We have to get out of here, right now."

She complied as I helped her up and out of the compartment. That those long lovely legs had been somehow compressed into that space seemed as impossible as the old one-thousand clowns and one car gag. Her white leather coat with the white fur collar and a green pants suit with ruffle-neck blouse looked remarkably fresh, but her hair was every which way. The innocuous brick structure of the rest stop was our backdrop, nothing to hint at the horrors within the men's room. She was stiff and I had to walk her over to the Maverick as gently as if this tall young woman were a little old lady. I guided her into the front seat passenger side, and came around and got in behind the wheel.

Luck was kind: nobody had pulled in here off I-80

to take a break or a dump or piss or any combination thereof in the vital seven minutes or so it had all taken. I had passed a larger rest stop perhaps twenty miles back where many trucks were parked, their drivers snoozing, but this stop was too small to accommodate more than a handful of semis, and we didn't have even one at the moment. Nice to catch a break.

I had to keep going east, needing an exit that would allow me to get off and come around to head back west to Iowa City, although I wasn't sure, frankly, if returning was such a good idea. Of course, I wasn't sure of much at all, right now.

The heat was going in the car, just at a comfortable warm setting, but Annette was shivering, even though she was bundled in that lined leather coat with its fur at the neck, long brown hair spilled over her shoulders. She had her seat belt on, but was hugging the door, leaning in on herself as if trying to assume a fetal position while sitting down.

"You want more heat?" I asked.

She shook her head. Her fists clenched each side of her coat, holding it to her by the lapels as if she were freezing, but she shook her head. That shivering didn't have much to do with the cold, I didn't think.

"I'm going to turn around as soon as I can," I said. "I'll head us back."

She nodded.

"Did they hurt you?"

She shook her head.

I just drove for a while. Maybe ten miles later I came to an exit, used it and then we were going west again. I still had the radio on, that easy listening station, but down so low you could barely make Dino out doing "Everybody Loves Somebody Sometime."

After a while, I glanced over at her and she wasn't shivering any more. Her askew hair nonetheless framed in a striking fashion the olive oval that held her beautiful features. She looked more relaxed, even a little sleepy.

I said, "I was coming out of the restaurant when I saw those two grab you."

She turned her head and gazed at me, almost as if noticing I was there. "What happened to them?"

I wasn't sure what to say. This was the daughter of one of the top mob bosses in Chicago, so the notion of killing shouldn't shock her; but then she'd just spent an hour or so stuffed into a car trunk, waiting to be raped and killed herself, so I thought I should err on the gentle side.

"I took care of them."

Her eyes tightened.

I returned my gaze to the road and the moonlit highway and the surrounding snow-patched landscape.

She asked, "Who are you?"

"I'm Jack, remember?" I glanced at her. "Are you okay? Did you take a blow to the head or something? Don't you recognize me?"

"Who are you *really*?"

I didn't say anything.

"You work for my father, don't you?"

I didn't say anything.

"What happened to those men? Did you...kill them?"

I didn't say anything.

"Did you, Jack?"

"...Yes."

She swivelled her gaze toward the road. "Good."

I was thinking fast, or anyway trying to. This had all been on the fly, and there'd been no time to waste cooking up a story for the girl, if I somehow managed to rescue her. Now that I'd pulled off that unlikelihood, I had no option but to improvise.

"I do work for your father," I said, "but I'm not one of his...whatever you call it."

"Soldiers?"

"Yeah. I'm not a mob guy."

"What *are* you, Jack?"

"I'm a PI out of Des Moines. I mostly do divorce work."

"Aren't you a little young for that?"

"I'm not the boss. I'm just an employee of the agency."

She was studying me. "Just an employee, for some private eye agency in Des Moines. Not a soldier, for my father back in Chicago."

"That's right."

"But you killed those two? Those big black fucking sons of fucking bitches?"

"I, uh...I was in Vietnam. Thought I mentioned that."

"Oh. Yes." Her eyes were on the highway now. "You did say something about that, to K.J. Sorry. I...I forgot."

"Under the circumstances, understandable."

We rode in silence for maybe a minute.

Then she asked: "You were watching me for my father? Why would he do that?"

"Oh, I don't know. Maybe he had the wild idea you needed protection."

You'd think that would have stopped her for a second, but instead she came right back: "Then you *were* watching me."

I thought for a moment. The closer I could get my story to the truth, the better it would play and the easier it'd be to maintain.

"No," I said. "I was watching Professor Byron."

Her face jerked toward mine, eyes and nostrils flaring. "Why?"

"I don't know for sure. I'm just doing a job."

"Tell me what you *do* know, Jack."

"Well…this is reading between the lines. I'm just a grunt in this war. But I think your father wanted me to gather evidence showing what a louse your prize professor is."

"*What?*"

"I gathered photos of Professor Byron with another coed. And he's married."

She was sitting forward, shaking her head, which sent her long hair tumbling back into more or less its normal down-her-back configuration. "Are you kidding? I told you before, at Sambo's—I know all *about* K.J. He's a free spirit. I don't love him, not *that* way."

I could have been a stickler for accuracy and reminded her that she'd been blowing the dude in his study the first time I saw them together. But she was running short enough a fuse already.

"Yeah, I get that," I said. "I understand. But your father, and I've never met him, but knowing what generation he's from, my guess is, he assumes you would be shocked and appalled by the professor's lecherous activities. I mean, these guys from the Depression and World War Two, they have a whole different way of looking at the world. Sex and love are interchangeable to them. The idea that a nice girl like you could admire your professor and want to collaborate with him and also go to bed with him without being in love with him, without wanting to spend your life with him, *and* not caring how much action he's getting on the side…well, that just doesn't fly with that crowd."

"And yet my father has fucked more showgirls than Sinatra."

That would be a lot of showgirls.

She was saying, "My father is completely immoral, no make that amoral, where sex is concerned, but he's got that same goddamn double-standard as the rest of the men of his generation. Madonnas and whores, that's women to him."

"Not to make too fine a point of it, but I doubt he thinks of you as a woman at all."

"What?"

"You're a girl. His little girl. And this professor is betraying a teacher's trust and abusing daddy's precious dainty child."

She laughed and something harsh was in it, surprisingly so. "If you only knew what you were saying…."

Well, I didn't. I was just filling the emptiness in the car, and trying to convince her I was on her side.

We drove silently again, maybe for five minutes. Then I noticed her sitting up, her brow furrowing.

"My God," she said. Her brain was starting to work. "There are dead men back there at that rest stop."

"That's right."

Wide eyes fixed on me. "What are you going to *do* about it? What am *I* going to do about it?"

"Well, we can't go to the police."

"Why not—wasn't I kidnapped?"

"You were, but the way I handled it was not... strictly kosher."

"You...what *did* you do?"

"I'm not going to give you the details."

"You mean you...pretty much murdered them."

"Pretty much."

She sighed. Leaned against the door again. "I don't know if I believe you...."

"Oh, I murdered them."

"Not that." She shrugged. "I buy that easy enough. What I doubt is you're just some PI from Des Moines, not one of my father's soldiers."

"Do I look like one of your father's soldiers?"

"No. You...you look like a soldier, though."

"Did I mention Vietnam?"

"You mentioned it. Are you taking me to my apartment?"

"I've been thinking about that. How shaken up are you?"

"How shaken up would you be?"

"Fairly shaken up. You said you weren't hurt, but they grabbed you, treated you rough, taped you up and threw you in that trunk—you must have aches and pains."

"You could say I have aches and pains."

I watched the road. We were coming up on the Quad Cities. "I think we should get a room somewhere and let you rest up and kind of heal up."

"Why? What's wrong with my apartment?"

"Your apartment, across from the Sambo's where two black thugs kidnapped you, couple hours ago? That the apartment you mean?"

She said nothing, but she was holding onto her coat lapels again, and despite her dark complexion looked very pale, though some of that was moonlight and dashboard glow.

I said, "I would like to talk to your father. Tell him what happened."

She turned sharply toward me. "I don't want to have anything to do with my father!"

"I can understand that. But those two dead guys from the South Side, they do have something to do with your father. He's in the middle of some kind of war with them and their black brothers. I want to ask him what to do with you, strictly for your protection."

"I don't want his protection."

"Would you rather I hadn't been here tonight? Do I have to paint you a picture of what kind of fun and games would've been starting about now?"

She said nothing, but then shook her head. "You're... you're probably right. In a case like this, my father is the person to talk to."

"You want to talk to him yourself?"

"No. He and I don't talk."

"Would it be all right if I protected your interests?"

She nodded, once, still clutching her lapels.

We crossed the Mississippi and before long I took the Highway 61 exit and drove down through Davenport all the way to the riverfront, crossing under the government bridge and pulling into the Concort Inn parking lot.

I was able to park near the entrance. "Look," I said, turning to Annette and resting a hand on the seat behind her. "Just so you know. We'll go in, I'll register us as husband and wife, Jack and Annette some-shit, and ask for twin beds. You have some fairly liberal notions about sex, but in case you're wondering, I have no intentions of asking for a reward or anything."

"I didn't think you were."

"Good. This is about not getting killed. You not getting killed, me not getting killed. Those are the goals."

"I can get behind those goals."

"Fine. Let's go in. If we get a twitchy desk clerk, I'll say the airline lost our luggage."

But the desk clerk didn't give a shit whether we had luggage or not. He was a little put off by me paying in cash since the hotel really did prefer credit cards, but that was all.

The room was not as nice as the suite the Broker had arranged for my last visit, but it was anonymously modern and clean and had a view on the river. Also, the twin beds I'd requested. I set my nine millimeter on the nightstand between us, to emphasize the seriousness of the situation, and also because I might need the fucking thing.

Then I realized I was still in that stupid jacket I'd bought at the truck stop, and took it off and threw it on a chair. I also got out of the black Isotoner gloves.

She sat on the edge of her twin bed facing mine almost primly, hands folded in her lap. She looked beautiful in that fashion model way of hers, dark hair stopping at the white leather shoulders on its way down her back, eyes as big and brown as ever, mouth as fully lush if sans lipstick; but with an edge of controlled hysteria about her.

"Jack....Do you mind if I take a shower?"

"No. Let me in there for a couple minutes, first, would you? I neglected to use the bathroom at that rest stop, having other business to attend to."

That actually made her smile.

So I went into the bathroom and I took a fairly major shit and emptied my bladder while I was at it; afterward, I turned on the ceiling fan, gentleman that I am, and splashed water in my face until I felt slightly alive. I mention all this not to share the fascinating details of my toilet activities but to demonstrate that I was giving Annette every opportunity to bail. She was alone out there, with my gun on the nightstand, with fan noise going behind the closed bathroom door, and I was doing my best to display trust. And to give her an opportunity to do the same.

When I emerged lighter and renewed, she was

hanging up her coat in the closet. She smiled at me. She seemed calm enough.

She said, "I guess I haven't thanked you."

"It's okay. I'll hit your father up for some kind of bonus."

She came over and touched my face. "You aren't as tough as you pretend. I have a feeling, underneath it all, you're a pussycat."

I smiled. "I guess you've got my number."

On the other hand, those dead assholes in the rest-stop john might've had a different opinion, if they'd still been in any shape to have opinions.

A terrycloth robe was hanging in the closet, with a CONCORT INN logo stitched on its breast pocket, and she took the robe with her into the bathroom and shut herself in.

I went over to the phone and had the desk put me through to the Broker's emergency number. Three rings this time.

"I'm at the Concort Inn," I said.

"What the hell are you doing there?"

"I'm in a room with our client's daughter. She's taking a shower. You wouldn't want to come over here and have a talk with me about what I've been up to lately?"

A long pause. *"I believe I would. What room are you in?"*

I told him.

"I'll get the key to another room nearby where we can talk."

"How long?"

"It may be an hour."

"Call from the lobby."

"All right. Quarry?"

"Yes?"

"What have you done?"

"I've done fine. You'll be pleased."

She came out of the shower, her hair in a turbaned towel, her nice shape wrapped up in that terrycloth robe. She came over and sat on the edge of her bed, facing me where I sat on the edge of mine, having just got off the phone.

"Why don't you take a shower?" she asked. "I feel like another woman."

I felt like another woman, too, but I said, "Only one robe."

"Don't worry about it. It'll be refreshing."

Hell.

I went in and showered. When I came back out with a towel knotted around me, all the lights were off and she was under the covers of my bed. But the drapes were open on the window onto the river and River Drive, so some flickery illumination came in and turned the room blue-gray.

Her hair, towel-dried and a little frizzy and lots of it, framed that model's face of hers; the covers were pulled up above her breasts but her shoulders were bare except for where her hair touched them.

She asked, "Don't you *want* a reward?"

I came over and said, "Who's that sleeping in my bed?"

She giggled; it did seem kind of funny at the time.

On the other hand, she was about half out of her gourd, after all she'd been through.

"You know," I said, looming over her, "your father, though I repeat I've never met him, hired my agency because he didn't like the idea of you sleeping around with your professor."

"You're not my professor."

"How do you know I'm interested? Maybe I'm gay."

She pointed to where the towel was pointing back at her.

"Touché," I said.

She giggled at that, too. I'm telling you, it was funny. I was wittier than Oscar Levant on the *Jack Paar Show*. You had to be there.

Of course, I *was* there, lucky me, and when she flipped the covers back, she showed off an olive-toned body that was perhaps more slender than to my usual taste, but those legs were as shapely as they were long and her waist was supernaturally narrow and the breasts, while small, got help from a prominent rib cage and had dark brown aureoles with nipples that were looking right at me, daring me to make something of it.

"Do me," she said, and parted her legs and in the midst of a brown thicket, pink glistened and I buried my face down there and made it glisten some more. She came quickly and hard, and then I was on my back on the bed and she was kneeling between my legs now, and she was very skillful, thorough and even loving.

She got on top of me after that, riding me with no mercy, her eyes rolling back in her head as she came again, just as hard; but we wound up with her on her back and us fucking frantically, as if our lives depended on it, those long legs kicking the air past me, and me rutting like a goddamn dog, as if we'd almost lost our lives together tonight, and hadn't we, almost?

For all that frenzy, the bang ended with a whimper as she began to cry and I felt my eyes tear up as I held her close and nuzzled and kissed her neck. Emotions were stirring in me, emotions I thought were gone. I hadn't felt like this since my honeymoon and I had thought I would never feel like this again, and hadn't really wanted to.

Then she trotted off to the bathroom again. I wiped myself off with my towel and leaned back against my pillow, propped against the headboard, and thought about Dorrie, sad, pretty Mrs. Prof. So far on this job I'd killed three guys and screwed two very lovely women. I'd done it all, in a very short time.

Everything except the job I'd been hired for.

The phone rang, and the Broker said, "I'm in 714, just down the hall from you."

"Okay," I said.

I got my clothes on and went over to the bathroom door, behind which water was running.

I said, "I'm going down to the front desk and get us some toiletries—toothbrushes and toothpaste and stuff."

"Okay!" she said.

"Won't be long."

In 714, the Broker and I sat by the window at two chairs on either side of a small round table with a built-in lamp, which was the only light going. His expression was stern. He wasn't staying long, judging by the camel's hair topcoat remaining on.

"I have to make this fast," I said, "or Annette will be suspicious."

"You're calling her 'Annette' now?"

"That's right, because she isn't Doreen or Cheryl or even Cubby."

This Mickey Mouse Club reference was lost on him, so I cut the comedy and filled him in, in short, brutal strokes.

Finally, he said, "You did well."

"Will you handle our client? And explain that I wasn't trying to discover his identity, that it just fell in my lap?"

"Yes. Certainly."

"Do it now. Tonight."

"Well, of course."

"I mean, we'll stay the night, Annette and me, and tomorrow morning I will need to know the game plan. Does her father want to send somebody to collect her? Do I go back to Iowa City and let her return to her apartment? And do we finally pull the plug on this cluster-fuck of a job?"

The Broker shook his head. "I believe our client will want you to attempt to complete what you've started."

"Getting a window to do that, where the stateroom

isn't jammed with coeds and wives and writing students, may not be a breeze."

The Broker shrugged and stood. "You'll do your best, I'm sure....We'll talk tomorrow, first thing. I'll let you know then."

I stood. "Okay. There's one other thing."

"What?"

"Tell the desk clerk I need a couple of those little traveler's kits—tiny toothpaste, toothbrushes, deodorant, and so on. Have a bellhop bring 'em up right away."

"All right. Why not just call down?"

"That's where I am right now, getting that stuff. Got it?"

"Got it."

When I returned to our room, Annette was still in my bed. The lights were off but for a reading light built into the headboard. Her face had a carved beauty, her Italian heritage giving her a Madonna look, despite our recent whore-worthy bed boogie.

She asked, "Do you mind if I sleep with you?"

"No."

"May be a little crowded."

"That's okay."

"I just…just don't want to sleep alone right now. I need somebody strong beside me."

"Well, I'll have to do."

She smiled. I was a card, wasn't I?

"Jack, where's our toothbrushes?"

"They had to go rummaging in a storeroom. They're sending the stuff up."

Right then came a knock—*thank you, Broker*—and

I gave the kid a buck and took the two little plastic bags of sample-size toiletries and deposited them in the bathroom. Then she was right behind me, in the Concort Inn robe, and first she brushed her teeth and then I did and it was as cute and domestic as could be.

I got in bed, and she got in after me and switched off the reading light, but we didn't close the drapes, liking the soft glow from the streetlamps and business signs and the river with Rock Island glimmering beyond. I had an arm around her and she was cuddled to my chest, like she was a tiny thing though she was almost as tall as I was.

There is something about being in a hotel room in bed with a woman with the lights out and nothing out there but the night that encourages a peculiar kind of intimacy. Like being at camp in a bunk bed in the dark and sharing with friends all sorts of hopes and dreams and secrets.

I said, "Can I ask you a few things?"

"Sure."

"Remember how I wondered if you were collaborating with the professor on your book?"

"Yes."

"And you said you weren't."

"Right."

"He was just helping you."

"Yeah."

"I don't want to upset you. Maybe this can wait. This can wait."

She sat up, leaned on an elbow, the big browns locked on me. "No. Tell me."

"I found something out, shadowing the professor."

"That he likes to fuck young women?"

"Well, I learned that, too. But...what kind of stuff are you dealing with in your book?"

"What...what do you mean, Jack?"

"I mean, there was something Byron said to you the other day, about you reporting every bad thing you ever saw or experienced with your father. What would that be, exactly?"

"Jack, I...that's kind of personal."

Not long ago, I'd been eating her out; not along ago, my dick had been halfway down her throat. And this was kind of personal?

"Honey," I said, trying that out, "I have a good reason for asking."

She sat all the way up. I did, too. But the sheets and covers were around her waist, so her small, pointy breasts were accusing me.

She said, "You know I have a rather...strained relationship with my father. Right?"

"I kind of gathered."

"There are...reasons for that."

"Reasons besides he's a drug trafficker and murderer?"

She half-laughed, half-sighed. "Yes. Yes. Other reasons."

"He beat you?"

"No."

"Then he...oh."

"Yes. 'Oh.' He fucked me, Jack. He fucked me from when I was twelve, around when my mother died, and until I was fourteen when he remarried and I got shipped off to boarding school. When I was older, later teens, when I was home for vacations or during the summer, there were no…advances, no sneaking into my room. He had a wife now and that was the past and it was never spoken of. Like it never happened. But it did."

"Christ. I'm sorry. How does a thing like that…?"

"My mother died. Of cancer. It was lingering. In fact, the…abuse, the psychologists call it, began during Mother's illness. I became the woman of the house at a very young age, her surrogate in many respects.…"

Many respects was right.

She was saying, "I have terribly mixed feelings about it all, and—"

"Mixed feelings? What's to be 'mixed' about?"

"That's just the thing. The horrible, the most awful part to admit—I was his willing partner. Oh, I didn't like it at first, it hurt me, I was too small, but I knew Daddy loved me and that I made him happy and I was taking over for Mother. Filling in for her, taking her place. And as the months passed, I came to like it. I liked having orgasms, and I liked having closeness with my father, and I became a kind of second wife to him."

"I don't understand."

"Neither did I. Only, after he married, and our relationship stopped? At first, I know this is sick, this is crazy, but I was jealous. And I told a priest, and the priest secretly, taking a big chance, got me psychiatric help, and I came to know how wrong it was, how sad and sick and awful it was, and became very ashamed."

Yeah, you got to hand it to psychiatry. Really put things right, that crowd.

"And the priest and the shrink, they didn't report your father?"

"Daddy is a big contributor to the diocese. And as for my psychiatrist, well, you know who my father is. What would Daddy have done to that doctor?"

Hired somebody like me.

"Anyway," she said, "I know now, intellectually and emotionally, that my father is a terrible man, a sociopath. I want nothing to do with him."

"And you're putting this in your book?"

"Yes. Yes, of course."

"Aren't you afraid of the repercussions?"

"What can Daddy do about it? Kill me?"

Well, he'd fucked her, hadn't he? Why was killing her out of the question?

And this was it, wasn't it? The secret that Lou Girardelli could not allow to get out. A book about him could contain all sorts of speculation about the mob and criminal activities; that kind of occasional bad publicity came with the territory, and even built a guy's legend. But a confirmed story, from his own daughter, of incest and abuse?

I put my hands on her shoulders and said, "You don't know what you've got yourself into, Annette."

She shook her head of hair the way a lioness does its mane. "Of course I do. I'm going to free myself and became an artist, a real artist, through my book."

"Your non-fiction novel."

"Yes. My non-fiction novel."

"Thanks to the instruction and nurturing of Professor Byron."

"That's right. Absolutely right."

How could I tell her that her latest father-figure was fucking her in a whole new way?

Maybe just give it to her straight.

"For all I know," I said, "the book you're writing may be a masterpiece. But even so, I discovered something very troubling about Professor Byron."

"Please. You're not…come on. *Jealous*, Jack?"

"No. Did you know the professor was writing his *own* book about your father?"

She smiled. Laughed. Shook her head. "No he isn't. You're confused. He's helping *me*."

"He's pumping you." Boy was he pumping her. "He's got all this juicy stuff about your father committing incest with his underage daughter, and that's going to make his non-fiction book a huge bestseller…" If it didn't get him killed first.

She was frowning now, and shaking her head again. "No. No, Jack. This is crazy."

"I swear to you, Annette. He's been researching your father for several years. This is his big follow-up to *Collateral Damage*. He already has a publishing contract. He isn't collaborating with you—he's *researching* you."

Her mouth dropped open and her eyes were wide as well. But thoughts were flickering behind those eyes, as defensiveness and denial gave way to everything fitting into place.…

Finally she said, damn near shrieked, "That *bastard!* That fucking *bastard*...."

I took her by the shoulders again, held tight. "I know this is a shock, but you have to get past it in a hurry. What the professor did to you isn't even the worst thing that happened to you tonight."

Breath poured out of her and she swallowed and, those huge brown eyes locked on me but half-lidded, she nodded.

She asked, "What now?"

"You get some sleep. I'm going to help you."

"How?"

"I don't know yet. But I will."

"What about calling my father?"

"I'll handle that."

"Can I *trust* you, Jack?"

"You can."

The crazy thing was, I wasn't lying.

TEN

At some point I'd gotten up and peed and shut the drapes, and we might have slept deep into the morning if the phone hadn't rung. Both of us were startled awake, and I was sleeping next to the nightstand and reached for the phone, though my hand initially touched the nine millimeter's cold metal skin. Then I found the receiver and it was the Broker.

"You're to take Miss Girard back to Iowa City, to her apartment," Broker said, after perfunctory hellos. *"She's to stay in for at least today. No meetings with Professor Byron or anybody else for that matter."*

"That would help me out," I said, purposely vague, "if you intend me to pursue that other matter."

"I do."

"Okay, but shouldn't I stay with her? I have a hunch there may be other black guys on the South Side who could find their way to her apartment."

"Have breakfast at the Concort coffee shop," he said. *"Make a leisurely exit from the hotel. If you leave no earlier than ten, then by the time you reach Iowa City, the girl's father will have representation there."*

By "representation" I took it to mean that guys with guns would be sitting in the apartment house parking lot. Hopefully white guys.

"Okay. But Miss Girard and her father aren't on the best of terms. I'm not sure she will go along with that."

As you might imagine, my nude bedmate was sitting up by now, leaning on an elbow, her eyes perked with interest and her nice little breasts just plain perked.

"Whatever their differences," he said, *"they have a common interest in this matter—specifically, keeping her alive."*

"Not a bad point."

"But I would like you to have her call her father so they can discuss it themselves. Perhaps come to a meeting of the minds if not a reconciliation."

"Got you. Right here from the room? This phone okay?"

"No. Have her use one of the booths in the lobby. I don't care to have a long distance call of that nature billed to the hotel."

"Fine. But I have a couple of concerns of my own."

"The kind you can't speak about in front of Miss Girard."

"Bingo."

"Well, we'll have a chance to talk. For now, take a shower, have a nice breakfast, and head back to Iowa City."

"Sure."

We said perfunctory goodbyes, and I said to her, "That was my boss at the PI agency back in Des Moines, who your father hired me through. We'll be heading back to Iowa City and, for the time being, you'll have bodyguards provided by your father."

She frowned. "What if I don't want bodyguards provided by my father?"

"Well, I guess that's up to you. But I killed two soul brothers yesterday, and if I kill any today, I'll forfeit my NAACP membership card. It's an associate membership, but still."

She smiled. The absurdity of the situation was such that joking about murder played pretty well.

"I understand," she said softly. From her expression I could tell she'd come to some sort of decision. "But I want to talk to my father, myself."

"I want you to. My boss wants you to. Your father wants you to. So it's unanimous."

"Should I do that now?"

"I was advised that you use a phone booth. We don't want to leave a trail."

"Any other instructions from your boss?"

"We're to have a shower and then some breakfast."

Eyebrows went up over half-lidded brown eyes. "Alone or together?"

"What?"

"The shower? Alone or together?"

"I think that's our call."

So we showered together. Because she was tall, it was tricky—not the showering, the fucking—but we were both motivated enough to make it work.

Back in the same clothing as yesterday, we felt a little grungy despite the shower, or maybe because of it, and in the Concort coffee shop, we took a booth in back where we could talk and not look conspicuous.

Not that we really looked conspicuous, but these were the same clothes I killed those guys in, and I did feel a little cruddy.

With morning sunlight pouring in the mostly glass walls of the corner-set restaurant, this being a new day was readily apparent, and she shook that fluffy, slightly frizzy brown mane as she interrupted sips of orange juice to say, "I can hardly believe it happened. Last night seems unreal, like something out of Jean-Luc Godard."

"What did he write?"

"He's a filmmaker. French New Wave?"

"All I know about the French is, they dig Jerry Lewis."

She made a face. "Well, they *are* a contrary lot, the French."

What was wrong with Jerry Lewis? Hadn't she ever seen *The Nutty Professor*?

But I never argue with beautiful women who fuck me in the shower, so I said, "You need to cooperate with your father."

"I will."

"Really?"

"Really. I will. I know my ass is on the line."

"And it's a really nice ass, you don't mind my saying, and I'd like to see it and everything attached to it stay that way. Nice, I mean."

Our breakfast came. I was having Eggs Benedict and she had French toast.

When I cut into my eggs and they bled yellow, she said, "*Ick*. How can you stand that?"

"The same way the French stomach Jerry Lewis, I guess."

"I never liked Eggs Benedict. It sounds like somebody who might work for my father."

That was pretty funny, and I gave up a smile. "Speaking of your father...please tell me he doesn't know about the book you're writing."

"He doesn't! Oh my God, how stupid do you think I am?"

"I don't think you're stupid. But you might be foolish."

"I am not foolish. I pride myself on my levelheadedness."

Sure. Like spending the night with a guy she knew jack shit about and humping him silly. After all, hadn't I rescued her from kidnappers? Kidnappers I'd murdered without qualms, which I assumed was a trait not shared by all of her boyfriends. That kind of levelheaded.

I swallowed a bite of the eggs; the hollandaise wasn't great, kind of vinegary.

"Your old man's not to know," I said. "Don't mention your book under any circumstances. If he asks about the professor, just say Byron has been helping you on short stories or something."

"Okay, but...some day he's going to find out."

"Right. If it's published—"

"*When* it's published."

"When it's published, he'll know...and probably won't be able to do anything about it. But keeping it from him till then may be tough. I don't know diddly damn about publishing, but don't they announce the books they're doing? Don't they do advance publicity?"

She shrugged. "If the publisher is discreet, Daddy won't learn of it until the review copies have gone out, and then it will be too late."

I held up a palm. "Okay. I can't help you with that. I don't know what he's going to do under those circumstances. But I do know, if he finds out now? He'll do something severe."

"Daddy wouldn't harm me."

No. He would just have sex with her when she was twelve and then have sex with her for another couple of years after that, and screw her up psychologically so bad that she was capable of levelheaded judgment like checking into a hotel with a hired killer just because he looked like a college student and was pleasant after he murdered people.

"Well," I said, "he'd harm your *book*. He'd grab you just like those spades did, and hold you until his people have found every manuscript, every carbon copy, and destroy them all. If copies are in New York, you'll read and hear all about a major office building where a whole floor got taken out by an electrical flare-up resulting in a most unexpected fire."

She said nothing. She ate a bite of French toast.

"You're not disagreeing with me," I said.

"No."

"Good. You be discreet. Anybody else on campus know about this project?"

She shook her head. "Just K.J."

"And he won't have told anybody, since all he's doing is stealing from it."

Her olive complexion paled. "It's so hard for me to believe…that K.J. would *betray* me like that. I thought we were artists! Fellow artists."

"I don't know much about artists, but I do know they are self-centered egomaniacs who don't give two shits about any other artist."

Her full lips formed a tiny smile, touched with just a little maple syrup. "For somebody who doesn't know much about artists, you could write a book."

"Maybe I will someday."

That amused her. "Will I be in it?"

"No. You can trust me for my discretion."

After I paid the check, I ushered her into the lobby and then walked her to the bank of phone booths and she slipped into one. She'd be reversing the charges, so we didn't need to go get change from the front desk or anything.

While I was waiting, a hand touched my shoulder and I whirled and damn near cold-cocked the Broker, who bobbed his head back in momentary alarm, then said, "Easy, my boy. Take it easy. We only have a few minutes, perhaps seconds. What is it we need to discuss that we haven't already?"

I took him by the elbow and we crossed to a pair of soft chairs in a waiting area. I leaned forward and so did he, the light-blue eyes unblinking and looking almost gray today, possibly because of his gray-vested suit.

"I may be new to this business," I said, "but I know all about loose ends."

He said nothing, just barely nodding.

"Am I in any danger?" I asked. "Are *we* in any danger?"

He didn't pretend not to know what I was talking about. His white eyebrows rose a tad, his thick white mustache wiggled just a little.

Then he said: "It's true that we've wandered off course in this affair. That we've severely broken protocol. You are not supposed to know who our client is."

"Yeah, and our client isn't supposed to know who I am, either."

Another tiny nod. "But none of that was our doing. And I think the gratitude of our client, for your gallantry where his daughter is concerned, cancels out any concern we might have that our client could consider us, as you say, *loose ends* that need…snipping."

My gallantry, huh? Killing those soul men in a rest stop shitter, and banging the client's daughter in a room in the Broker's hotel. Who says chivalry is dead?

"Okay," I said. "But if anybody with spaghetti sauce on his tie gives me a funny look, he's had his last fucking meatball."

"Understood."

"And, Broker—if some people die who maybe weren't scheduled to die, you need to know I was protecting our asses…*capeesh*?"

He smiled a little and nodded. "By all means, protect us at every cost. One can always find another client. A young man with your skills, Quarry, is a rare find."

He sounded like that fat guy in that movie about the Maltese falcon, right before Chubby sold out his sidekick.

But I said, "Just so we understand each other."

"We do."

I got up and went one way and the Broker got up and went another.

When Annette stepped from the phone booth, I asked, "Everything all right?"

She nodded. "He says he's concerned for my safety, and insists that two of his people position themselves outside my apartment. He wanted two more *in* the apartment, but I convinced him there just wasn't room."

Plus, there seemed to be no access to that second-floor apartment other than the front, open stairway, so another pair of bodyguards would have been overkill.

"That's all?" I asked. "You were on with him for quite a while."

"I know. We did…we did argue about something."

"What?"

"He wants to come to Iowa City himself, tonight. To see me. He's worried about me. He says he wants to make it up to me. Make amends."

"And you said no."

"I said no."

"And he's coming anyway."

"Yes."

On the drive back to Iowa City, I encouraged her to find a radio station of her choice; she turned the dial to classical. That stuff gets on my nerves, but I didn't say anything. She needed settling down worse than I did.

The trip back, which didn't take much more than an hour on I-80, she spent grilling me, but in a nice enough way. She had spilled her lovely guts to me yesterday, and now she felt like turnabout was fair play.

So I gave her the story of my life. I won't repeat this conversation because you've heard it all before, only you got the unexpurgated version. I let her know about Vietnam and my cheating bride, but left out minor details like crushing that asshole Williams under his car and turning to hired killing as a way to re-enter the civilian population and make a meaningful contribution.

The car waiting in the little apartment complex across from Sambo's was a dark blue late '60s Thunderbird with a vinyl top. They had taken a spot off to the left as you faced the building, and I pulled into one nearby.

I got out and looked at the two guys, a mustached, pockmarked little weasel at the wheel and a huskier pockmarked big weasel on the passenger side; both wore pastel leisure suits with turtleneck sweaters and had greasy black hair plus the usual mutton chops and their mustaches drooped like they were auditioning for an Italian western.

I leaned at the window of the huskier guy and he powered down the glass.

"My name is Jack. I'm taking Miss Girardelli up to her apartment, but then I'll be going out for a while. I may be back later."

He frowned. "Why you tellin' me this?"

"Mr. Girardelli sent you fellas, right?"

"And this concerns you how?"

"This concerns me that you know which side I'm on, so I don't wind up with an extra navel."

Then I went around to Annette, where she'd got out of the Maverick, and walked her up the wrought-iron-railed cement stairs. I got the nine millimeter out of my waistband to go in and take a quick look. Her apartment was furnished in low-end contemporary stuff, probably came that way, with the only signs of Annette the many books stacked here and there, and some posters on the bedroom wall—Albert Einstein sticking his tongue out, Ernest Hemingway in a sailor hat, a couple others I didn't recognize, one a woman who was definitely not Raquel Welch, who would have been my choice.

The place was clear, closets and all. Before going out the door, I gave her a little kiss that she turned into something bigger, but I left it at that and made my getaway.

My original plan had been to utilize the window provided by standing up Dorrie Byron for lunch to finally dot the professor's I, but that no longer seemed wise. Better to go collect those photo prints, which I did in downtown Iowa City, and then keep the meeting at the Holiday Inn coffee shop, which I also did, after showering (alone) and changing my clothes.

Turned out I wasn't hungry enough to eat, after the big breakfast, and ordered an iced tea while Dorrie, having no appetite either, asked for a cup of coffee.

Frankly, she looked older than before, and I didn't think it was because I'd been hanging out with a younger woman. Her attractive face had a puffiness,

particularly around the eyes, which were red-rimmed.
She was in a white blouse with pearls and a black skirt
and black pumps, all of which complemented her figure
and her legs and everything just fine. These were still
eminently jumpable bones.

But her face was a mask of tragedy.

I'd barely settled in the booth when I asked her, "Are
you okay?"

"Not really."

"You saw your husband, didn't you?"

She nodded, and her chin crinkled.

"Didn't go well?"

"At first, just fine. He let me cook for him. He let
me…service him. I even stayed the night. That way he
got breakfast out of me. We even showered together."

That gave me a chill. A little too weird, that.

I said, "And?"

"And then he told me—it was over. He wants a
divorce. He said he was glad I'd stopped by and that
we'd been able to make 'one last bittersweet memory.'
But we were over. I told him…well, you know what
kind of things I told him."

Her voice was hoarse enough to make it obvious
that many of those things had been screamed.

She was stirring her coffee. She'd been doing that
when I got there, I never saw her put any sugar in, but
she kept stirring. And her eyes were staring past me.

My iced tea arrived, but I didn't touch it.

She said, "He didn't care. He didn't care about losing
half or more of his money. Or losing one or both of his

homes. He didn't care. He didn't care about losing me, at all. He was going to be very rich from his next book and I wouldn't get any of that, and he would be able to start over, and at the top, he said." Now she looked at me. "You know, it might not hurt so bad if he'd told me straight out, when I first got there? He shouldn't have had me cook for him. He shouldn't have let me make love to him."

"No. That was bastardly, all right."

"Bastardly. Good word for that bastard."

"I have the photos for you."

"Please."

I got out the yellow packet, having already pulled the Annette photos, leaving only those of the little blonde behind. And of the little blonde's behind. Charlie the dead PI had got some great shots through those gauzy curtains; perfect for *Penthouse*.

She flipped through the prints, glassy-eyed, like a poker player on a losing streak who just knew no winning hand was coming.

She asked, "You know this girl's name?"

"I can get it."

"I'll...probably need it. For the divorce proceedings, and..." She reached out and gripped my left hand with hers, its diamond ring catching the light. "Jack, you've been wonderful. Very professional, and I...I feel we *had* something, you and I."

Well, I'd had a really good time. Beyond that, I couldn't or shouldn't say. I merely nodded and smiled and that vagueness was plenty for her.

Then I said, "You need to go home, Dorrie. This time, you really do need to go home."

She nodded. "I have to check out."

Then she slid out of the booth, pausing to say, "Can you get this? Put it on the expense account?"

"Sure," I said. I didn't have an expense account, but a well-stirred cup of coffee and an undrunk iced tea wouldn't break me.

I decided today would be the day. With Dorrie on her way home, and Annette holed up in her apartment, I should finally have my opportunity. I headed back to the split-level on Country Vista on an afternoon turned colder, with some icy teeth in a wind desperately looking for snow to blow around but finding the white stuff too frozen over to comply.

So confident was I that I actually loaded up the Maverick in the driveway down behind the split-level, piling in my sleeping bag and space heater and the little TV Charlie bequeathed me and a few leftovers from my 7-Eleven runs, and runs was right, when your regular diet was Slim Jims and Hostess.

When I returned to my window, the house was cold enough without the space heater for my breath to show. I sat like an Indian and looked out at that cobblestone cottage, just waiting for my moment. I had on a black sweatshirt and blue jeans over long johns and the corduroy jacket and the black Isotoner gloves and the nine millimeter was on the carpet next to me, since this goddamn job had been just one unexpected thing after another.

Maybe six-fifteen, with night here already, I saw the

professor coming out from behind the cottage to go into the little unattached cobblestone garage. From within, he opened the double-door, a big slab of gray-painted wood, and then I could see him getting into his maroon Volvo and backing out. He stopped in the drive, got out, closed the garage door, got back into the Volvo, pulled out of the drive and headed down Country Vista toward the main drag.

I was sitting up straight, the nine millimeter in my gloved hand now.

Finally an opportunity had presented itself, and I went out the back way and once again trotted down to cut through woods to where I could cross the street and come up unseen behind the rear of the cobblestone cottage. The gun in my waistband but my jacket unzipped, I followed my breath to the back door of the cottage. That was the only bad thing: I needed to get in without the professor noticing on his return that the door had been jimmied.

The rear door was old but the lock was new, the kind you could open with a credit card. But I didn't have a credit card, as that desk clerk at the Concort Inn could tell you. Trying to think of what I might use instead, I absently tried the knob and the goddamn thing was unlocked. The professor, for all his east coast sensibilities, had fallen for the Iowa hi-neighbor trustfulness. The sap.

From peeking in windows on my previous visit, I already knew the layout: a small unremodeled kitchen in back, wooden cabinets with counter and an old stove and 1950s vintage refrigerator and yellow Formica table; a pantry and laundry room next door; then, as you came from the kitchen, a study and a bedroom to right and left respectively; and a good-size living room with a cobblestone fireplace, which was going nicely, red-and-blue flames snapping as if its owner were in attendance. In this surprisingly expansive open-beamed space was a lot of dark wood paneling that dated back to when the cottage was built. A very rustic interior, with built-in bookcases in one corner and a braided throw rug and a green sofa with a broken-down look and a big captain's table under the glow of a hanging light fixture shaped like a yellow upside-down tulip.

I decided to get a head start on it, and went into the study. For half an hour, I went through his desk, its drawers and the file cabinets. I gathered every damn document that had the name "Girardelli" or anything vaguely Italian or having to do with Chicago. I was feeling pretty proud of myself, looking at a big stack of manuscript pages and carbon copies and boxes and notebooks resting on his swivel chair when I heard the back door open, and then close.

Positioning myself to the left of the door, snugged between the frame and the file cabinets, I waited and listened, the nine millimeter in hand, its snout up.

Out in the kitchen, he was setting something down. Then I heard him open the door on the refrigerator and stuff was going onto wire shelving, and then cabinets were opening and cans and other things were getting set down on wood. He'd gone to the store. He had to eat, didn't he? Well, actually, he didn't, but he didn't know that.

I couldn't think of any reason not to pop him there in the kitchen and was about to step out and do that very thing when somebody banged at the front door, hard, and I damn near pissed myself.

Hugging the wall again, I heard him saying, "Now what the hell...."

I knew the feeling.

I heard him cross into the living room over the wooden floor, the footsteps different on the braided rug, then the door opened and he said, "*Dorrie!* I thought we'd settled everything."

I knew the feeling!

The door slammed behind her.

"Almost, darling," she said. "Tell me, though. We did have something, didn't we? Once upon a time? Isn't that what you storytellers say? Once upon a time?"

"Dorrie...of course we did. For that part of my life, for all those years, you were the only woman, the most important person in my entire life...."

Why was he talking so quickly? Why did he sound so goddamn desperate?

"That's nice to hear," she said. Her voice had an odd wistfulness, and a distance that was much farther away than from the study to the living room. "It does help, darling. It does help."

"You need to put that down, Dorrie! Put it down right now!"

If you ever watched the old sitcoms on TV, like *I Love Lucy*, there was always this audience member on the canned laugh track who said, "*Uh oh!*" at a key story moment. I wasn't watching a sitcom exactly, but I heard that familiar voice. *Uh oh* was fucking right....

Then came a sharp crack, almost as if the fire had popped, but it wasn't the fire, was it?

I was hoping I didn't have to kill her. I really didn't want to, and I stood there frozen in my tiny space between door and filing cabinets, hoping to hear that door slam as she went away, having done my job for me.

But I didn't hear the door slam.

I heard a second sharp crack.

And when I finally went out there, she was curled on the floor next to him, a certain elegance about how she lay there, as opposed to her husband, still in a tan jacket from going to the store and chinos and pretty much looking like a pile of laundry dumped by a fed-up housewife. And maybe he was. Her blouse was crimson and the stain on the white fabric grew where she'd shot herself through the heart the dead prick had broken. A little revolver was in her limp hand. Byron had taken his in the forehead and his talented brains were leaking out the back of his skull.

I leaned down for a look at the gun, and it was Charlie Koenig's .38! I'd put it in my suitcase but Dorrie must have helped herself to it when she visited my room. Her using that weapon would add another nice confusing layer to any police investigation.

The gunshots had seemed small if distinct. Nobody lived across the street now, not even me or the late Charlie. The cottages to left and right were spaced well away. I did not feel anyone was likely to have heard anything suspicious enough to call for investigation.

Wasn't much left to do but burn those manuscript pages and notebooks in the fireplace. It took a while, and as the flames ate the opus, its author—dead and sprawled on the floor by the wife whose spirit he'd killed—basked unknowingly in their dancing reflection.

ELEVEN

A space was open next to the dark blue Thunderbird with the Illinois plates, and I filled it with the Maverick. Both my car and the goon squad's were backed in, for a good view of the little red-brick apartment building and its modest parking lot.

Whenever I'd done surveillance on Annette, over the past several days, I parked across the way in Sambo's semi-enclosed lot; where the Thunderbird was parked made it too easy to come up on them from behind. But I guessed Girardelli's boys knew their own business.

Right now the Thunderbird had only one pock-marked weasel sitting in it, the heavier-set one, on the passenger side.

I came around and bent at his window; his droopy-mustached, suspicious face had followed me over and his eyes were glittery slits under thick eyebrows. His leisure suit was a pastel green, his turtleneck a slightly darker shade with a gold chain necklace nestling in sweater folds. Whatever happened to black-and-white pinstripe suits with black shirts and white ties for the hood about town?

The craggy-faced weasel powered the window down and said, "Mr. G is up with his daughter. He said you should go up there."

"Okay. What happened to your partner?"

He nodded toward the restaurant down and across the way. "Sal's over having a bite. We take turns."

"That parking lot's where they grabbed the girl last night."

"You don't fuckin' say."

"You and Sal might not want to split up. If the spades send reinforcements, taking you fellas out one at a time would be a way to go."

"Do I look like I was born the fuck yesterday?"

For all the gunk on his hair, he might have been born the fuck a few seconds ago.

But I said, "Hey, just trying to help out."

"You can help out by going up there like Mr. G said."

"No problem." I smiled and nodded.

He glowered at me and powered the window up and turned his eyes toward the building.

I took the steps to the exterior landing along which apartment doors were lined, motel-style, and I knocked at Annette's. She answered right away, cracking the door, then undoing a night latch and letting me in. Looking pale and a not a little shell-shocked, she was in a black zippered top with pointed collars and black-and-white geometric-pattern bell bottoms, possibly the ones she'd worn that first night when I saw her go into the professor's cottage.

Annette basically had two decent-size rooms and a bathroom here, the living room (which you entered into) taking up two-thirds of a long narrow area, the back third a kitchenette. The bedroom and bathroom were off to the left. These were not lavish living quarters, but in a college town, for a student, this was as good as it got—Annette lived alone with easily twice the space any double-occupancy dorm room would provide. Probably set her back two hundred bucks a month.

This pad, and her hip threads and that white Corvette, meant Daddy was still signing checks to and for his Darling Girl. And his Darling Girl—despite Daddy using her for a fuck toy when she was twelve—was still letting him underwrite her lifestyle and her education. She'd get cut off, no doubt, when her tell-all book came out; but Annette probably figured she'd be making her own way in the world by then.

A rust-colored couch was at left as you came in, a framed Warhol soup can over it—a framed pop art print was on the opposite wall, too, a panel out of a love comic book—and a big portable TV was sitting on a metal stand in the corner at right, angled so that couch sitters and a big overstuffed rust-color easy chair at right could take in its impressive 25 inches. Another example of Daddy's love?

Speaking of Daddy, he was seated in that easy chair next to an end table with a remote control, a lamp with a Tiffany-style shade and a tumbler of what looked to be Scotch on the rocks resting on a coaster. I recognized him at once, since he'd been in many a national magazine and on the nightly news plenty of times.

Still, I was surprised by how small he was. He couldn't have been more than five eight, and maybe weighed 140, despite a modest paunch. Like his boys, he wore a leisure suit, a money green one with a yellow shirt with pointy collars and a gold crucifix on a gold chain dangling in graying chest hair, bridging fashion and religion.

Very tan (he had a place in Florida), Lou Girardelli was probably late fifties but appeared older, with that shrunken look people in their seventies can get; his hair was cut short, no mutton chops for him, and was salt-and-pepper, emphasis on the salt. His face was oval like his daughter's but his nose was hooked and crowded by dark little eyes behind goggle-lens glasses with dark green frames.

His smile was friendly enough as he got out of his easy chair and extended his hand, approaching me.

Annette, uncharacteristically timid, was saying, "Jack, this is my—"

"Jack!" Girardelli said in a sandpaper baritone, as we shook. "Nice to finally meet you. I spoke to your boss in Des Moines, of course, but you and I haven't had a chance to talk ourselves."

He was keeping to the PI story I'd fed Annette, whether from information the Broker gave him or what his daughter told him, I couldn't say.

"No, we haven't, sir."

"Come, sit, sit." He gestured to the couch and I sat and he played host, extending his arms as if this were a castle and he its king. "What can we get you? Annie has Scotch and bourbon and—"

"Nothing, sir," I said, with a mild smile and an upraised hand. "I'm fine."

"You're sure? It's no trouble."

Not for him. It was Annette who'd have to play bartender.

"You're very gracious," I said. "No."

Annette smiled, tightly, joining me on the couch, but not right against me, not too cozy. Her hands were folded in her lap and she sat very still and stiff and straight.

Girardelli shrugged, and rather than return to his easy chair, joined us on the couch, sitting next to his daughter, putting her between us, and she scooched somewhat closer to me.

"I'll always be grateful to you, Jack, coming forward to help Annie last night." He rested a hand on Annette's shoulder. Her flinch was barely perceptible.

He was saying, "Those moolies would have done Christ knows what to my little girl."

"Wouldn't have been pretty, no."

"Animals. A bunch of damn animals. There's going to be a bonus in it for you, Jack."

"I appreciate that, sir, but it's not necessary."

He was studying me, smiling. But the eyes behind those oversize lenses bothered me. They were small and hard and cold, like black buttons sewn on a doll.

"I just stopped by," I said, "to make sure everything is cool where Miss Girardelli is concerned. That she has proper protection, which I can see she has."

He patted Annie's leg, just above the knee; she closed her eyes. "No one's going to touch my daughter, that I promise you. Sal and Vin are two of my best men, and another team will be in by midnight. They'll work shifts, and I may even bring in a third team."

"Good. How long will you keep that up?"

"Well, an indefinite period. Not long. Not long.

We're dealing with our little Mau Mau uprising back home in our own way, on our own turf."

Annette said to him, "Daddy, I don't want to live in a bubble. I need my space, and privacy."

Christ, she sounded about twelve.

"Sweetheart, no one will bother you. My boys will stay out of your way, but they're here if you need them. I'm gonna stay tonight myself, right here on this couch."

Annette closed her eyes again. The hands in her lap were fists.

"Sir," I said, sitting forward, "I think you should know, I've taken care of our *other* business."

"Good! Good!" The genial smile broadened but the eyes stayed just as dead. "I am going to make sure you get something extra for this quality work. If you ever get tired of the private eye business, Jack, I can find a place for you on my personal security staff."

"You're kind, Mr. Girardelli. But I do think I need to get going." I rose. "We're a small agency and there's always another job waiting...."

He nodded, then he got up and said to his seated daughter, "Jack and I are going to step out for a few moments, Sweetheart. I need to talk to him."

She smiled tightly. "Sure, Daddy."

I said, "There's a restaurant across the way."

"All right." He went to the door, opened it and gestured for me to go on out. "We'll get coffee."

I smiled at Annette and she smiled at me and rolled her eyes as kids have forever done behind the back of a parent.

"Be good," I said.

And she nodded, and smiled again, the young woman smiling, not the twelve-year-old.

So once again I sat in a booth at Sambo's, this time with one of the top mob bosses in Chicago. I had a Coke and he had coffee with lots of cream and sugar. In the bright glare of the relentlessly illuminated pancake house, I could see every freckle and age spot and wrinkle and stray facial hair on that too-tan puss, every blackhead and tiny red vein and enlarged pore on that hooked honker. His eyebrows were out of control with lots of white twisting around black, and his teeth were too white, too big, probably purchased.

"Do you smoke?" he asked.

It was the first thing he'd said since we left his daughter's apartment. We'd nodded to his boys in the Thunderbird (both weasels were in the front seat now) and just walked quickly over. I had my corduroy jacket on, but he hadn't put his topcoat on, and it was bitter.

Now, in the warmth of Sambo's, in a world of orange and brown and white and stainless steel and glass and faux-leather, the Chicago mob boss was seemingly asking for my permission to smoke.

But I'd misread him, because when I said I didn't smoke, he said, "Good. I don't, either. I gave it up, three years ago. Causes cancer, you know, that's no joke. I can see you're a clean-cut boy. Vietnam?"

I nodded.

"Your Broker, he likes ex-GIs. I don't blame him. You're dependable. You don't scare easy. You can think on your feet."

Right now I was on my ass in a Sambo's booth, but I was thinking, all right. I was thinking that those dark eyes behind the green-framed glasses were like a shark's.

We had good privacy, nobody in an adjacent booth, and we spoke softly but clearly.

He said, "What happened to that fucking prick?"

"If you mean Professor Byron," I said, "his wife murdered him this evening. Sick of him cheating on her with this coed and that. Then she killed herself."

The eyes suddenly got lively, gleaming, like water pearling off gun metal. "Excellent. Nicely done."

Was it my fault he jumped to the wrong conclusion?

He was saying, "Sure you wouldn't like to work for me, Jack? Maybe you didn't want to say so, in front of Annette."

I said, "I'm happy working for the Broker. But I do apologize for...well, I know you like being insulated from people like me. And with all due respect, sir, I prefer insulation from people like you. From any client —that's our mutual protection, after all."

He nodded. He was smiling but not showing his expensive teeth. That tan was damn near black; fuck cigarettes, he'd get skin cancer if he kept that up.

I asked, "How are we with the trash I dumped on I-80?"

That meant the two black kidnappers.

He said, "Right now it's still classified a robbery. I believe within twenty-four hours, it'll be a gangland killing. But that doesn't mean it'll come to my doorstep."

"Good."

"I mean, these niggers are always killing each other. They got more factions than the fucking communists. And, like I said, my people are busy killing black asses even as we speak."

I nodded. "I was improvising, sir. I certainly didn't mean—"

He raised a benedictory hand. "No. You did well. You saved my daughter. Nothing's more precious to me than my little girl." Then he sat forward. "What about the prick's book? That fucking manuscript?"

"Assuming he didn't send a copy to an editor in New York or somewhere, it's gone, all of it. I had plenty of time in his study and I burned every goddamn page, every scrap, every note."

He sighed. "Wonderful to hear—excellent work, first-class, Jack. But that bastard was close to Annette. Could she have a copy?"

"No, I don't think so."

He sipped his coffee, thought for a few moments, then shrugged and said, "You must understand, Jack, that Annette and I have had our differences."

"That's hard to believe. You seem so close."

Another shrug, more elaborate. "It's these times. These fucking draft dodgers, these dirty damn hippies, and that's just the start of it. Think of that professor, and the trust he betrayed! I'm paying that university for my child's education, and one of their staff is… is….I can't *say* it. It's disgusting."

"Yeah. Kind of turns your stomach."

The wild eyebrows climbed high, even above the goggle glasses. "Problem is, Jack, my generation, we had it tough. We survived the Depression. We survived World War Two, you know?"

What I knew was, Girardelli had gotten rich in the Depression off bootleg booze and brothels, and spent the war stateside and out of uniform, getting richer, selling black-market meat and tires and counterfeit ration stamps.

"Yeah," I said. "Moral decline. It's a pisser."

He nodded vigorously. "Well, our problem was, we spoiled our kids. Wanted to give them what we couldn't have, wanted them not to have to live through any of the tough times we suffered through."

I was drinking Coke. Somehow I managed not to do a spit take.

Girardelli was saying, "So I don't blame Annette. She can't help it that, when she was little, I spoiled her little ass. I gave her everything a father could, and more."

That was for sure.

"Anyway, she's a wonderful girl, and very talented, really gifted, you should see the poetry she wrote in finishing school." He shook his head and let out a weight-of-the-world sigh. "But she's of her times, it's these *times*, she's one of these *kids*, wild and free and rejecting the old values, rejecting her own *father*, sometimes."

"Kids today."

He leaned forward. His sandpapery voice got a little

rougher. "So it's possible she was helping that prick with his book. Possible. Possible. And maybe, just maybe, she has a carbon copy or some shit."

"I guess that's not beyond the realm of possibility."

He was almost purring now despite that rough-edged voice. "She likes you. She trusts you. Jack, I don't mean to get personal, but did you have relations with her?"

"I won't lie to you, sir. I kissed her."

He threw up his hands. "She's a beautiful girl. I don't blame you." Then he leaned in again, buddy buddy. "What I'm asking is, could you stay on and get closer to her? Just for a day or so? You can search her room. Or you can get her out of that apartment, and *my* guys can toss the place."

"Well…maybe. I guess."

"I can offer you ten thousand on top of all the other money, and it goes straight to you. Never mind your Broker. And if you turn up a copy of that manuscript, well, I'll double it."

"Well…I could do that, I guess. Who couldn't use ten grand? Or twenty?"

"Good. Good!"

"But, sir—one thing does concern me. As I mentioned, normally I would be in the dark about all this— I wouldn't know you, the client; I wouldn't know about manuscripts and…it does worry me."

"Why? How?"

"You maintain a degree of safety by requiring those levels of insulation we talked about. I don't want to be a threat to you. I don't want to be seen as a loose end.

Or the Broker, either. You need to know I'm loyal. I'm discreet."

I watched his eyes carefully as he responded.

"Jack, I know how to reward loyalty."

His smile was winning, almost charismatic. The smile wrinkles around his eyes were convincing, too. But those eyes. Those black-button eyes. Those shark eyes.

He left a ten on the table on top of the check, and we headed outside. The night had grown colder and darker, the moon lurking behind cloud cover, and I put on my gloves. We came along the side of the restaurant, and I went ahead a few steps and pointed.

"That's where they grabbed her, sir," I said.

And I walked over to the spot. Only a few cars in the lot, and no people but us.

He came over.

"Really, Jack, it doesn't matter," he said.

"Actually, it does."

The .357 magnum came out of my pocket in a flash of shiny silver and I slapped him alongside the head, its long, thick barrel colliding with bone and tearing flesh. His knees buckled and he went down, not unconscious but stunned, a pile of meat in a green leisure suit. I kicked him in the head and *now* he was unconscious.

The Sambo's lot might stay empty only a few seconds, so I had no time to waste. At the street, I waited for a car to pass, then trotted across and over to the apartment house parking lot, and came up along the rider's side of the Thunderbird.

The heavier-set pock-faced weasel was behind the wheel again, and I startled him a little. I leaned in and grinned at him and made the roll-the-window-down motion, even though I knew the windows were electric, and when the glass was no longer between us, he said, "You scared me for a second, you dumb shit," and I shot him in the head.

The other weasel jumped a little as his partner's brains splattered him in the face like a cream pie, and he hadn't had time to get over it when I shot him in the head, too, that bullet going through and taking some brain and blood to splash and streak the now spider-webbed rider's side window.

Then I trotted over to the Sambo's lot, where Lou Girardelli was just coming around, pushing up on one hand.

"What the fuck," he said, blood streaming down his face from where the .357 barrel's sight had torn his flesh. The dead little eyes had some life in them, for once. "What the *fuck*, Jack?"

"Just tying off a loose end, Lou," I said, and fired once and the dead little eyes were dead again.

I was wearing the Isotoners so I didn't need to wipe off the handle of the .357 I'd taken off Charlie back at the rest stop, and just tossed it near Girardelli's body. He was on his back and the entry wound was about the size of a quarter and the seepage under his skull was something I was careful not to slip in as I left the lot to cross the street.

One more loose end to deal with.

I kept my head down in case any of the apartment

tenants were peeking out their windows after hearing sounds that could have been shots. The nine millimeter was in my waistband and the corduroy jacket was unzipped as I went up the cement stairs.

After I knocked on Annette's door, I said, "It's Jack!"

She cracked the door, then opened it, her eyes wider than I'd seen them and I'd seen them pretty damn wide.

I stepped inside. "Your father's dead. I'm sorry."

She said nothing, her hand splayed to her mouth.

"They got the two downstairs, too," I said, "then took off, fast."

Her eyes somehow got even wider, moving side to side now.

"I don't think you're in any danger, not with your daddy dead. But I can't stay."

Now they narrowed. "Oh, please, you *have* to—"

I put a hand on her arm. "Honey, I'm not really a PI from Des Moines. I do freelance work for guys like your father, and if I stick around, I'll be hip deep in shit."

"You lied to me?"

"If I'd told you I was just another soldier, how would you've reacted? I have to go."

What, did you think I was going to shoot her in the head, too? What kind of prick do you take me for? She didn't know anything. She couldn't hurt me.

She was shaking her head, overwhelmed. "Will I... see you again?"

"Someday," I said.

Maybe a hundred years from next Tuesday.

I touched her face, and slipped out. She was just a silhouette in the doorway, then, and not even that for long.

Some first job. Six kills but not the guy I was hired for. Two beautiful women and more sex than I'd had in the last six months. I'd survived it all, but hoped this shit wasn't typical. I wanted to live a while.

It was a risk, removing a client before getting paid. But killing Lou Girardelli's ass was only prudent, in this case, and anyway, the Broker did enough business with Chicago that they'd surely pay off for their associate, so tragically and brutally murdered by those black bastards from the South Side.

As I headed west on I-80, toward Cedar Rapids to turn in my rental car and catch the next plane north, I had a pang or two about Annette. She'd have some rough days ahead—I'd left her with dead Daddy and his just as dead goombahs in her lap, and then there'd be the news about the murder/suicide at the cobblestone cottage. But she'd get over it.

Hadn't I left her a hell of a last chapter for her book?

THE
END

Get Hard Case Crime by Mail...
And Save 43%!